INTO THE DARK

Also by Nicholas Wilde:

Sir Bertie and the Wyvern
Huffle
Death Knell
Down Came a Blackbird
The Eye of the Storm

INTO THE DARK

Nicholas Wilde

Camera Journal
Cambridge 2021

Into the Dark

978-1-9168846-0-1

First published 1987 – Collins
This hardback edition 2021 – Camera Journal

camerajournal@hotmail.com

Cover and interior designed by Paul Sutton

One

'Can you see it yet? It *can't* be far now! Promise you'll tell me when you first see it!'

'Of course I'll tell you, Matt. It'll be another ten minutes yet, I should think, though how I'm supposed to find my way about with all these twisty roads I can't imagine. It's like the back of beyond.'

Matthew swallowed his rising excitement, yielding his body to the tug and thrust of the car as his mother tackled the bends. Then he leaned his head on the half-open window to his left, closing his eyes against the inrush of August air. The rattle of household goods in the cardboard boxes behind him was swept away and he strained his ears outward into the dark. Perhaps he would hear it soon. Smell it.

'You'll get ear-ache, love.'

'No I won't. You couldn't get ear-ache from this sort of air. It's so clean.'

'It's air just the same.'

'London could be millions of miles away, couldn't it?'

'It probably is, the hours we seem to've been driving. Push the window up, there's a good boy, I can't think what my hair looks like.'

The glass knifed its way upward and chopped the wind dead. In the back seat, the crockery and saucepans began to chatter again.

'Can you see it yet, Mum?'

'I can't see much at all, not even another car. You wouldn't think it was 1987, would you, these roads are like years ago. There hasn't even been a signpost for ages, we could be anywhere.'

'No we couldn't. This is the road all right, leading us straight there. I can feel it.'

A wave of excitement propelled him forward, and he fumbled among the maps and sweets in the glove-compartment until his hand found what it wanted. The paper slipped from its envelope with an important rustle and crackled open under his fingers. He clutched it in his lap and read from memory, staring out ahead into the darkness.

' "*Malham Cottage, let on a weekly basis for the Spring and Summer season. £70 per week including electricity. All conveniences. Everything provided.*

"*Malham Cottage is set in the extensive grounds of Malham Hall, in the village of Malham on the North Norfolk coast. Unspoilt countryside and immediate access to Malham Creek, the saltmarshes and sea.*

"*Key available on arrival from Mrs Weaver in the adjoining cottage.*" '

'Thank you, love, that's only the tenth time I've heard it since we started out. It won't get us there any quicker, you know.'

'Yes it will.'

Yes it would. For weeks he had felt the same secret thrill every time he'd spoken the words aloud. *Malham Creek. The saltmarshes.* They were a magic spell. It was as if the very sound of them brought the strange, unknown places nearer. Gently, he slid the paper back into the envelope and returned it to the dashboard, sealing it away with a click.

His mother reached out and squeezed his hand, more to reassure herself than him, he felt. He sensed her mounting nervousness.

'I hope it's all right, Matt. I'm almost beginning to wish I hadn't seen the advertisement. I hope you won't be disappointed. It's not like Southend, I shouldn't think, it's only a village and there won't be many people and ice-creams and things.'

'That's why it'll be nice.'

'I thought you liked Southend?'

The alarmed note in her voice put him on his guard.

'Oh I do, Mum, it's great. But this'll be a change, that's all. Different.'

The memories of daytrips to Southend crowded in on him again, the only holidays he'd ever known. She had gone there for his sake, he knew, so that he could say at school that he'd had a holiday like the others; if it hadn't been for him she would have been glad to stay at home, to put her feet up after a full week's work. How could he tell her now how he'd hated it? The long coach-ride early on Saturday morning, then on foot along the promenade past the screaming rattle of the games-arcades. Clinging to her hand as his only anchor against the surge of bodies and noise and heat and smell. Sick with fear that she would loose her hold and leave him; sick with the ice-cream that he knew she couldn't really afford; and, worst of all, having to smile all the time, until his face hurt, in case she looked at him to see if he was happy. Perhaps it would have been different if he'd had a father. Perhaps she wouldn't have had to try so hard.

Cautiously he reached up and eased open the window to a finger's breadth. The cool air rushed in against his ear and Southend was whistled away into the past.

'It'll be different all right, Matt. There's still not a soul in sight anywhere. Oh well, never mind, we'll find things to do. I'll take you down to the beach.'

'It's probably miles if it's the other side of the saltmarshes, and you're on your feet all day in the canteen. You always say they're killing you. You just have a good week's rest-up. Don't worry about me, I'll be OK.'

'Well, we'll see. It seems a funny idea, really, living in somebody else's house. I don't know if I'll be able to get used to it.'

'Lots of people do it. Lots of people at school rent places every summer.'

'It still seems funny. I mean, why should anybody want

strangers traipsing all over their house?'

'For seventy quid, probably. Hey, I wonder if anyone'd fancy living in ours for a London holiday? We could offer it cut price.'

His mother chuckled.

'We'd have to. We'd have to pay *them* seventy quid, I should think, for putting up with it. I can just see the ad: *Number 73 Byron Rise, luxury holiday council flat, immediate access to three square foot of garden and washing-line. All conveniences thrown in free, including noise of next door's dog, and Jim and Rita Parkes arguing half the night underneath.*'

'Well *I* like it.'

'Oh it's not so bad, I suppose. You get used to your own things. That's why it's so funny leaving it all behind.'

Matthew grinned, turning his head in the direction of the heaving boxes on the back seat.

'You must be joking! We've brought most of it with us!'

'Well you never know with these places. It says everything's provided, but people've got different ideas. And, anyway, I don't fancy using other people's stuff. It mightn't be clean. I'm going to give it a good going-over when we get there.'

'Oh Mum, this is supposed to be a holiday!'

'That's why I want to enjoy it. I can't enjoy it till I've got things straight. I only hope we don't have to boil the drinking-water. Molly from the canteen says *they* always do when they go to Spain. Anyway, I've brought some tummy tablets in case.'

'Oh honestly, Norfolk's not exactly abroad, is it?'

But he knew how she felt. Her nervousness and his own tingling excitement were one and the same. It *was* like being abroad in a way, after all – an adventure, sleeping away from home for the first time in strange surroundings, a first step into the unknown.

Soon, now.

The whine of the engine and the backward thrust on his

body told him they were going uphill, not steeply, but gradually and steadily. The low gear thrummed through him, increasing the pressure on his ears and the thrill of tension in his spine. In a moment they would be at the top. He held his breath, preparing himself for his mother's cry, for the lurch in his stomach which would signal that the final barrier had been crossed, that the end was in sight. *Can you see it yet? Promise you'll tell me when you first see it!* In every nerve of his body he knew that the cry would come.

In the next instant, it came, jolting him upwards as the car leapt over the ridge, suspending him weightless above the scene he had dreamt of.

'The sea, Matt! It's the sea!'

He thrust himself forward against his seat-belt, clenching his eyes.

'Tell me what it's like! Tell me! Describe it!'

'Oh, it's so grand, Matt! Big and grand, and right far out. So different!'

'What sort of different?'

'Well, just different. From Southend, I mean. So empty. I've never seen anything like it, it's that peaceful.'

'What colour is it? Describe the colour!'

'Not blue. More grey, really. Bluey grey. And light, Matt, much lighter than it is up here.'

'Tell me some more!'

'It's big, it goes all the way along on the other side of the rushes, all the way from left to right with the lights of the village in front. We're going straight down towards it.'

'What does it *feel* like from up here? Describe what it *feels* like!'

'Oh, love, I *have* described it. You know I'm no good at describing.'

Hardly perceptible below the excitement, a sob caught at her voice. Matthew sank back in his seat, his eyes still closed, and controlled his panting chest. Then he swung himself towards her and buried his face in her shoulder.

'That's great, Mum! Thanks. Fast now. Really fast downhill. Straight towards it!'

The old Austin sped seaward. In the back seat the last memories of London jostled and chattered for attention in their cardboard boxes, but their efforts were drowned in the roar of the engine. Then a shudder of gears and a left-hand turning, swivelling him sideways, and the downward thrust was over. They were on level road.

'It's the village, Matt. There's the first houses coming up soon on the left.'

He lifted his head, speaking close to his mother's ear.

'What's on the right?'

'Nothing. Nothing but the rushes, and the sea far out.'

'Stop the car.'

'But it might take a while to find it. We don't want to be late.'

'Please! Just for a minute.'

The tyres swished to a stop and the engine juddered into silence, a silence so sudden that it took the breath away. Without a word, Matthew unfastened his seat-belt and stepped out.

'Don't go away from the car, mind.'

For a whole minute he remained where he stood, arms crossed against the roof, eyes pressed shut, facing outward to the last of the light. A smell of salt and seaweed drifted inland on the air. There was no sound anywhere but the wind and the rushes, and far off, farther than anything he'd ever known, the long cry of a gull, which was the spell of the sea.

He smiled. It was real, then. Malham Creek. The salt-marshes. Places conjured up inside him for so long by the touch of the letter and the sound of the words, until they had become part of him. But he was here now, like part of them. In everything about him there was a note of welcome, like a long-awaited welcome home.

'Come on, Matt, we can't keep Mrs Weaver waiting up.'

He turned away and settled himself back in the car. The engine broke the silence.

'You *were* right, Mum. It isn't a bit like Southend.'

'But it's all right, isn't it? You're not disappointed?'

'Disappointed? You're joking. It's just what I knew it'd be. Perfect.'

'Still, don't talk too soon. We haven't seen the cottage yet.' But her voice sounded pleased and hopeful.

'That'll be perfect too. You wait.'

The car pulled forward towards the village and soon the pitch of its motor changed, tense and hollow, echoing back from between the houses. Suddenly Matthew frowned.

'Have you told Mrs Weaver, Mum? About me, I mean?'

'Well of course I have, in my letter. I told her there'd be the two of us.'

'But did you tell her what to expect? So she won't get the jitters when she sees me?'

'Oh I'm sure I did. And it doesn't matter anyway. Gracious me, there's nothing for anyone to get jittery about.'

He turned his eyes aside and stared blankly into the darkness, wondering. Wondering whether his mother was right. Whether people in Norfolk were used to the blind.

Two

Light and darkness, these he could distinguish. But only as shadows, grey shadows on the back of his eyes, no more. Day-shadows and night-shadows. And sometimes, brief and unexpected, blurred outlines, ghosts of denser grey, trees and houses, figures in the sunlight; but whether of things half seen or merely half remembered, he couldn't tell. Still, they gave the doctors and the teachers at his 'special school' hope. "Just one more little operation, Matthew, and we may be lucky, you never know." No, he never knew, not for certain. And so he put it from his mind as best he could, not daring to hope too much, happy to make friends with the world in his own way, with ears and nose and fingers.

'Oh dear, we're here, love. There's a sign on the left in the bushes. "Malham Hall and Cottages." '

The car seat tugged him sideways then bumped his stomach upward.

'What's it like?'

'I can't see yet, it's a sort of driveway by the looks of things.'

The tyres munched on gravel, spitting out the stones at the base of the car.

'Blimey, Matt, this can't be the right way, can it?'

On both sides the swish and squawk of branches on the windows whipped the cardboard boxes into a frenzy of excitement. Matthew slid himself forward again to the dashboard, reading the darkness with his ears.

'It *is*. I'm sure it is if it said it was. It's just a bit overgrown, that's all.'

'You can say that again. Gracious knows what these branches and things are doing to the car.'

'Just doing us a favour, probably, and scratching the rust off.'

'That's cheerful, there was nothing but rust in the first place. – Oh no, hold tight!'

A soft snapping of stems and they were at a standstill.

'What's the matter? Are we there?'

'No, the driveway's forked in two.'

'Which bit of the fork are we on?'

'We're not on either bit. We're right in the middle with the bonnet stuck in a great load of nettles or something.'

'Is there a sign?'

'Not as I can make out. There's nothing but these daft bushes. And it's getting that dark. Now what are we supposed to do?'

'Well we've only got two choices, haven't we? So it's not *so* bad.'

'Thanks, you're a real comfort you are.'

But beneath her attempt at laughter lay a note of increasing tension and uncertainty. There was a long moment's silence, filled only by the unsteady throbbing of the engine and the little sigh her dress made when she craned her neck from side to side.

'Oh I don't know, Matt.'

'Which way looks more likely?'

'It's a bit wider to the right, I think. I suppose we'd better give it a try.'

The gear lever grated into reverse and with a high-pitched whine of protest the Austin was forced to retreat. Another stop, another metallic rasp from somewhere in the bowels of the engine, and the tyres ate their way slowly forward again over rising ground. By the time she next spoke, her voice was almost lost in the thresh and squeal on the windows.

'This can't be right, it just can't be! And it's not even wide enough to turn round!'

The sounds of gravel receded and were replaced by other noises, the thump of wheels in potholes and the lurching creak of axles. Matthew clung to the dashboard, his whole body shaken empty of breath. Beside him, he could feel his mother's struggle against the steering-wheel at every rut, could hear it spinning free in her hands, first one way then the other, as if it had taken on life of its own. She was sweating.

'It's OK, Mum, it'll be OK if you go slow.'

'I'm going as slow as I can. – Sit *back*, Matt, will you, for goodness' sake. I've told you a hundred times.'

The edge of panic in her voice sharpened his own nerves. He fell back, protecting himself against the potholes by clutching at the sides of the seat.

'And hold on to those boxes for me, there won't be a cup left to drink from.'

But even as he released his grip to turn round, the brakes threw him forward. With a violent jolt behind him, one of the boxes toppled. Saucepan lids clattered and rolled, then lay where they were on the carpet, pulsating faintly with the motor. His mother's dress swished, there was a click of the ignition key, a judder from the engine. Then silence.

When he spoke, his own voice sounded loud and unnatural. He dropped it to a whisper.

'What is it, Mum? Is it the cottage?'

'No, it must've been the other fork. We've gone wrong.'

'Where are we then? Where have we come to?'

'It's a huge sort of garden, with the driveway running all round it.'

'But where does it lead to? It must lead to something.'

'It does, Matt. Over there, on the other side. It's the Hall.'

He didn't move. He sat where he was, one hand on the seat, the other tensed on the dashboard, listening to the excitement in his chest. Then he reached for the handle on his left. The door gave way and swung heavily outward, bouncing slowly into stillness. He turned his head.

And for a brief instant, one of those rare, unexpected instants when outlines seemed to take form from the mists of his vision, he saw it. Only a blur, a vast, dim rectangle against greyness, a shadow against shadows. But the windows shone clearly, row upon row of them, glowing with rich brightness from within. A tremor ran through him, half joy, half fear.

His mother leaned awkwardly across him and wrenched the door shut with a slam. The building faded.

'Oh well, let's hope this doesn't disturb everybody in earshot.' At the touch of the ignition key, the car leapt into deafening life. 'We'll have to try the other turning and hope for the best.'

'But couldn't we go and ask at the Hall? To make sure of the way? They're still up.'

'No they're not, it's later than you think – it's nearly quarter past ten.'

The Austin threshed a wide arc through long grass.

'Are you sure, Mum?'

'Sure of what?'

'That they're not still up?'

'Of course I am, I can see they're not. The whole place is as black as the grave.'

As the car plunged once more into the tunnel of branches, Matthew swung round in his seat and stared back. But there was only darkness.

'Aren't you ready yet, Mum?'

'Hold your horses a sec, I can't face Mrs Weaver looking like this. Just one more minute won't hurt now we're here.'

They were there. And his mother was pleased and excited. The two cottages had been no more than a few hundred yards up the other lane of the fork, and they were lovely, she said: very small, and joined together, with lights in the windows on the right. So theirs must be the left-hand one, with flint walls and a porch. Only one window downstairs and two above, tiny windows with criss-cross glass.

He strained all his senses through the open door of the car. A radio nearby, muffled by the thickness of stone; and from farther off, deep in the distance, another sound, soft and constant from seaward.

The rushes.

Beside him, the powder-compact snapped shut, puffing out a wraith of scented dust. Then another scrabbling in the handbag, followed by a desperate swishing and tugging. His mother reached across and the teeth of the comb bit into his own scalp, crackling slightly in the stillness.

'There, that'll have to do. Now where's my cardie?'

'You *are* pleased, Mum, aren't you? It's all right, isn't it?'

'I've told you, it's as pretty as a picture, what I can see of it.'

'Describe it again.'

'Oh Matt, I *have*.' Her voice was absent and nervous as she fumbled in the back of the car, twisted round in her seat. 'It's lovely, just like an old-fashioned calendar.' He smiled, wondering what an old-fashioned calendar was like. 'Here it is, it's a bit creased up but it'll do for round my shoulders. I've got that many butterflies in my tum they could write a book about them.'

'Me too.'

He heard her stretch up again and crane towards the driving-mirror.

'Blimey, Matt, I look a real fright to be going anywhere.'

'You're not going anywhere, Mum, you're here. Anyway, don't worry, you'll always look the same to me. Just great.'

There was a silence, and he felt a tight squeeze on his hand.

'Come on then, love, we're all set for our big adventure. You wait here by the car and I'll go and get the key.'

He stepped out into the cool darkness and listened to his mother's footsteps retreating across grass. Her shoes ticked onto stone and he heard the buzz of a doorbell. He held his breath. The voice on the radio swooped downward into silence as if startled by the disturbance; then a door opened. He grinned: his mother's voice again, but different; her 'posh' voice. And then another voice, older than he had expected, and gentler. Mrs Weaver.

The sounds came slowly towards him: his mother's apologies

about “the lateness of the hour” and “the twisty nature of the journey”, and the murmur of sympathetic replies. Then:

‘This is Mrs Weaver, Matthew.’

He held out his hand in the direction of the voices and felt it clasped softly in the darkness. He had been right. An old hand, worn and swollen at the knuckles, but friendly, the sort of hand his grandmother might have had.

‘I’m pleased to meet you, Matthew. And I’m sure you’ll enjoy your week here in Malham. There’s so much to see.’

He forced out an answer through a sudden tightening in his throat.

‘Thank you.’

So she hadn’t been told.

The hand released its hold and was replaced by the more familiar one of his mother, worn and rough like the other, but plumper, with the thin band of metal on the wedding finger. He felt three little squeezes, the code they had adopted between them, unspoken and unexplained, yet clearer in its message than any words could have been: a secret message of comfort. He turned and gave his smile of ‘Message received’.

Together, they followed Mrs Weaver’s voice towards the door.

‘I’m sure you’ll find it to your liking, my dear, all the other visitors have loved it. It’s only small, two little bedrooms and a bathroom upstairs, and just the hallway and one room down below, with the kitchen built on at the back – that’s the only modern addition apart from the furniture and bathroom fittings, the rest of the cottage is kept just as it’s always been. It’s well over two hundred years old.’

‘Oh, how lovely. I love old things.’

‘Is Byron Rise an old property too?’

His mother’s fingers gave a nervous wriggle before she answered.

‘No, not what you’d call old, exactly. It’s quite a modern residence, in fact, compared to this. But it’s quite nice.’

A jingle of keys echoed in the hollowness of the porch.

'Well, here we are.'

The front door swung inward and there was the snap of a lightswitch, filling the world with grey warmth. 'This is the hallway. Come on in and I'll show you round downstairs. – And welcome home, both of you.' Her voice receded into the sitting-room and more lights clicked.

With a tremble of almost unbearable excitement Matthew felt his feet being guided across the threshold and his hand placed on the edge of the open front door. His mother spoke in a whisper by his ear.

'You wait here by the door, and I'll go and have a look round. Then we'll get the stuff out of the car when Mrs Weaver's gone. You're just in the little hallway. The sitting-room's down there on the left and the stairs are straight ahead. But don't move, not for a minute, till we get to know it, there's a table over by the wall opposite, with a vase on. – Oh it *is* going to be fun, Matt, it's all *that* pretty!'

The hand returned fleetingly to settle on his. Three squeezes, and she had gone.

He remained motionless and unbreathing, eyes closed, back pressed to the open door. The two voices faded through the sitting-room towards the kitchen, one explaining where things were, the other bubbling with genuine pleasure, its poshness already abandoned. So it was all all right.

Still he held his breath. Somewhere deep in the woodwork of the door behind him he could hear his own heartbeat. He smiled. Perhaps it wasn't his own heartbeat at all, perhaps it was the heartbeat of the cottage itself. Perhaps it had longed for him as he had longed for it, waiting for this moment of meeting.

Now!

He took his first breath, and they met. As his shoulders rose against the door and his chest expanded, the air that was Malham Cottage rushed into him, filling him with its presence.

Then he turned his head away towards the darkness, grinning, and wiped his sleeve across his eyes.

It was as he had dreamed it would be, the smell of comfort and homeliness and welcome. And, more than anything else, the smell of oldness, the gentle oldness of wood and stone, strange yet familiar, like a breath from the past. Everything was going to be all right.

A kettle was being filled in the kitchen. Mrs Weaver's slow tread approached again through the sitting-room, heavier on one foot than the other, the painful tread of the elderly. It would be nice to have her so near. Perhaps he could visit, perhaps they would become friends. He wondered whether his mother had told her.

Behind him, her dress rustled out into the hallway and stopped.

'Oh there you are, dear, your mother's just getting a cup of tea. What are you doing? Looking at the last of the light?'

The old panic caught at his throat.

'No, I'm. . .'

Suddenly angry at himself for his own embarrassment, he controlled his chest and tightened his hold on the door. Then, with one movement of his head, he turned to face the light and smiled.

For an instant which seemed endless, there was nothing but stillness. He held the smile bravely then felt it tremble away. The stillness broke. He heard her sharp intake of breath, the backward movement away from him, the unsteady hand stumbling for support on the opposite wall. The scrape of a table. The vase rocked for a moment, first one way then the other, over and over, and then hung suspended in silence.

The crash of its falling exploded in the hallway as the steps scuffled past him, out into the night.

His mother was there.

'I *told* you, Matt. I *told* you not to move! Where's Mrs

Weaver? Was she here when it happened?'

'Yes. No. Oh I don't know.'

'How did you do it?'

'I didn't! It was an accident!'

'But how did it happen?'

'I don't know. I don't know! It was an accident!'

'Why couldn't you do what you were told? I *told* you not to move! What were you doing over there?'

'I wasn't! I didn't! I don't know!'

Sobs choked him and he slid to the foot of the door, hiding his face in his hands. Then his mother's arm was round him.

'Oh I'm sorry, love, I'm sorry. It's all right. I'm just in a state, that's all. Look, it doesn't matter, we've had worse accidents, you and me.' A handkerchief dabbed helplessly at the back of his hands. 'Come on, it's all right now, and it's so lovely here. Don't let it spoil our holiday.' He threw his arms round her, burying his face in her shoulder. 'I'll pay for it, love. It's probably not worth much. I'll see Mrs Weaver tomorrow.'

'No!'

He pulled himself away, staring in panic.

'Why ever not, Matt?'

'No you mustn't! Don't talk to her about it! Don't ask her! Please! It'll only make things worse, it'll upset you, it'll spoil everything!'

'Whatever do you mean?'

'*Please!* Don't ask her! We'll leave the money here when we go. I'll pay, Mum, I'll pay out of my pocket money. You've got to let me! It was my fault, all of it!'

Three

He lay in bed with his hands clasped behind his head in the pillow, listening to the sounds of his mother from below. Quarter to midnight, she had said. She must be tired, but she wouldn't come up yet, he knew, wouldn't sleep until she'd got things straight.

This was always his favourite moment at home, the comforting safety of the blankets, the long wait for her approaching footsteps, her listening pause by his door, her nearness in the next room. And this was even better than their flat; her approach up the stairs would take longer, and her room here was nearer to his.

'Malham Cottage.'

He whispered the words aloud, confirming its presence about him, renewing their friendship. Only yesterday he had been lying like this in his own bed in London and speaking the same words, to conjure up this place like a dream. But now London was the dream and Malham had become the reality. He was here. It was as if he had been here always.

Then the other thought returned, tightening his throat.

It would all have been so perfect if it hadn't been for that. And it didn't make sense, it had never been like that before, in London. A fraction of a moment's silence sometimes, when he was introduced to new people, when they were told. Then they would find their voices again almost at once, and be too jolly, and speak too loudly as if he was deaf. But that was all. He had grown used to it, found it comical, laughed about it afterwards with his mother. But what had happened tonight in the hallway had been different. With a sudden sinking of the stomach he wondered whether everyone in Norfolk would treat him like that.

The idea frightened him. It just couldn't be true. Perhaps he'd been wrong after all, perhaps he was only imagining it. Perhaps she had just stumbled against the table because her legs were so old, and then been upset about the vase. He forced himself to remember, to summon back those terrible seconds. . . No, it hadn't been like that, it *was* different. She hadn't been upset, she'd been afraid.

He swung his head across the pillow again, away from the thought, fixing his mind on the final hour when the vase was swept up and forgotten.

It had been fun. Tired though his mother was, they had 'got to know' the place together, as they always did: the first tour with his mother guiding, holding his hand, touching things with him, walls and corners and furniture; 'getting to know' the stairs, and every room, especially the bathroom. His mother always set great store by 'getting to know the bathroom'. She was right of course. He smiled. There *had* been a few mishaps in the past.

Then the second tour, quite alone, with his mother watching. And it had all seemed so easy here. Not like some buildings he had been to, "enemy territory" as he called them, where everything was wrong, deliberately laid out to trap you, like a minefield: steps that cropped up in impossible places, angles of wall jutting out for no reason. But this he had managed almost at once, on his own. It was tiny, of course, and that helped, but there was more to it than that. It was "home territory", friendly somehow. He hadn't just guided himself, the cottage had guided him. Everything here was right.

He turned again.

Everything was perfect, except for that stupid business. . .

Suddenly the stillness was shattered by the doorbell downstairs. With a violent thumping in his chest, he pulled himself up on the pillow, straining his ears. The sounds in the kitchen fell silent, a startled, waiting silence. Then the doorbell repeated its summons. His mother's footsteps were crossing the sitting-room. He imagined her fumbling to untie her apron, as she always did when there was a 'visit', stuffing it under a cushion on the sofa on her way to the door. In the hallway now. Her whisper, so as not to wake him:

'Who's there?'

And another voice, directly below his window, a voice he knew well. A bolt was shot back. A few murmured words that he couldn't distinguish, then the door was clicked shut. He held his breath, hoping against hope that his mother's footsteps would return to the kitchen alone. But they didn't. Another slower tread was with them.

With a stifled cry of misery, he buried his head in the pillow.

'Matt, are you still awake?'

The voice was barely a whisper. He answered without turning towards it.

'Yes.'

Behind him, the bed creaked heavily downwards. The warm weight of his mother's body was against the small of his back.

'Did we disturb you?'

'It was Mrs Weaver, wasn't it? Has she gone?'

'Yes.'

'What's the time?'

'Way past twelve.' Her hand stroked the hair from his ear. 'Matt, why didn't you tell me?'

'Tell you what?'

'That it was Mrs Weaver who did it, who broke the vase.'

'Oh I don't know. Because I didn't want to upset you, probably.'

'You *are* silly, love. Why should it have upset me? She was the one who was upset, poor old soul, that's why she came round. I've never seen anybody more sorry. She's that nice, Matt, and that gentlehearted.'

'I know. That's why it doesn't make sense.'

'Why what doesn't?'

'Why she was so scared.'

'Oh Matt, she wasn't scared. Perhaps she was just startled, that's all, finding you there in the hall.'

'Buy *why*?'

'I don't know. She's old. Old people are a bit funny sometimes. You have to make allowances.'

'It wasn't like that. She was scared. She was scared of me.'

There was a long silence before her voice came again, close by his shoulder now. He could feel her breath on his cheek.

'I know what you're thinking, and it's just not true. You're thinking it was because of your eyes, aren't you? Well that's just silly. She didn't know. How could she have known? It doesn't even show.'

'It's not silly. If it wasn't that, it doesn't make any sense at all. Unless . . .' He swung towards her. 'Unless there's something else funny about me. Tell me! *Is* there?'

He heard the long tremor of her sigh and felt suddenly wretched about what he was doing to her. She was weary beyond telling.

'Listen, Matt. There's one thing we've always promised each other, isn't there? Do you remember? That we'll always tell each other the truth, you and me?'

A fleeting memory of Southend stabbed through him and he bit his lip.

'Yes.'

'Well listen then. You're a lovely looking kid, Matt. I can't think why with a fright like me as a mum, but there it is. You look as normal as anyone else, more normal than most and a darn sight better-looking. Everybody says so. I spend my whole time telling myself how lucky I am.'

A sudden wave of relief surged through him, and pity. He put his arm round her and grinned.

'Even when I knock milk bottles all over the floor?'

'Oh that's different. I could wring your neck then.'

Her chuckle broke the mood that had held them; he was glad to let the incident slip away, for her sake, to let their thoughts shift into tomorrow, a walk round the village, perhaps, if the weather was good, and tea in the garden at the back.

It wasn't until she pulled herself up to leave him that his anxiety returned. Hating himself even as he did it, he clutched at her hand and held her by him.

'*How* can you be so sure, Mum? That it wasn't because of my eyes?'

'Oh Matt, I can't go through it all again. I'm that tired I can't think straight any more. I want it forgotten. I just want you to believe me.'

'I do believe you. I know you mean it. I know you think it's the truth. But you can't be sure, can you?'

'Of course I'm sure. I've told you. I've never been so sure of anything.'

'But *why*?'

'Because that's what upset her so much, Matt. At what you must have thought. That's why she was crying down there in the kitchen. She didn't *know* you couldn't see, not till just now. Not till I told her.'

Four

Sunlight blew across the land from seaward. He could feel it on his cheeks as he made his way alone, exploring the path with his feet. Rough gravel all the way, with nothing to impede him, and grass on either side to warn him when he veered off course. It was 'his' path. Not far, quarter of a mile perhaps, and at the end of it his mother would be waiting, sitting on the low boundary wall which ran right round the grounds of Malham estate.

It had been her idea, after lunch.

'I've been thinking,' she had said. 'Before we pop down to the village, we'll go and have a bit of an explore round outside the cottage and see if there's a little walk you could manage on your own.'

The suggestion had stunned him. At home, on the fifth floor of Byron Rise, where the main road vibrated the windows even at night, the possibility of such a thing could never have been imagined. The walls of the tiny veranda had been the outermost limits of his independent world and he had accepted them without question. And outside those limits his independence had ended; he had surrendered it to the hand of his mother.

But after the first shock it was another feeling which had flooded through him, joyful and painful at once, a longing for the kind of freedom he had never even dreamt of, the freedom of a walk he could manage alone.

'I'm not saying there is, mind, but I shouldn't be surprised. It's that quiet here, Matt, and that empty, there'll never be a better chance.'

They had set off across the grounds to the south, moving gradually upward away from the sea and the village, with the wind at their backs. Just great open spaces of grassland, his mother had said, with a few clumps of bushes, and thickets of trees in the distance.

'It must all belong to the Hall, Matt. Blimey, fancy having all this for your garden – it puts our bit to shame all right. Not that there are any flowers or anything, it's all more like fields.'

But in spite of her cheerfulness his spirits had sunk with each step they had taken. The farther they went the longer the grass had grown, catching at his trainers and the knees of his jeans; and any attempt to keep his bearings by the direction of the wind had proved useless. By the time they had reached the boundary wall on the south, his hopes of coming this same way alone had faded. He could have been anywhere, drifting in windswept emptiness.

'Where are we, Mum?'

'As far as we can come by the looks of things. I can still make out the cottages with the tower of the church to their right, and then trees down beyond them – that must be where we came in last night. And more trees over to the left of us, with chimneys poking up. That's the Hall, I should think.'

He had forced out his reluctant confession.

'I don't think this'd be much good, for my own walk, I mean.'

'No, nor do I, and it's that hot. Still, never say die, that's what I say. Let's head back down to the cottage and explore round the back. There might be a pathway or something.'

And that was where they had found it. The gravel had begun only a few yards from the bottom of the garden and led in easy curves downward, towards the church. It had taken scarcely more than five minutes to reach the low boundary wall on the east, which was also the wall of the churchyard beyond.

'Oh Matt, it's perfect! It could've been made for you!'

They had followed it back up to the cottage again, then formally embarked on 'getting to know it': together the first time, hand in hand, then back to the starting-point. And there he had stayed, breathless with excitement, and counted a thousand, while she had set off once more alone, to wait for him at his goal. . .

The scent of lavender, humming with bees. Not far now, the last curve of the pathway. The bushes reached out to guide him and he quickened his pace, surer-footed than he had ever felt before. His mother's squeal of delight met him and he threw himself forward into it and into her arms.

'I did it, Mum, I did it!'

'You did, Matt! I knew you would!'

'I can come here whenever I like!'

'That you can!'

'And I could go on walking and walking for ever, couldn't you?'

She chuckled through the little tremor of tightness in her throat.

'I could, love, if it wasn't for these shoes.'

He fumbled at the roughness of wall and sat down beside her with the sun warm on his eyes. Somewhere nearby, an insect droned. There was no other sound but the familiar sigh of wind and rushes, which were part of the silence itself. He reached out for her hand.

'Thanks, Mum.'

'Don't thank me. It was you that did it. And anyway, it'll be a real treat for me knowing your feet are doing the traipsing about while mine are resting-up in the garden.'

'Are they very bad?'

'Oh I wouldn't say that. It's these shoes more than anything, they cut right across the big toe. Molly said it was daft to buy new ones, but I wouldn't be told. I should've brought the old ones with me really, but I just thought it'd be nice to look a bit smart on holiday, and they were such a bargain. I think they're more town shoes, though. They're a bit fancy for round here.'

'I bet they look great.'

'They did in the shop, before they had my toe sticking out of the side.'

A sudden thought crossed his mind.

'Look, Mum, don't worry about getting all the way to the sea or anything. It doesn't matter, I can always go for a walk along my path, can't I? That'll be just as good.'

'Well, we'll see. We might be able to get the car down there or something. Anyway, come on, I'm not a cripple yet. Let's go and have a nose round the village.'

Even before they had reached the north wall of the churchyard, Matthew could smell the tarmac beyond, rich and oily with sunlight. His mother steered him towards it along the narrow pathway through the gravestones, swinging at nettles with her handbag, then pressed him to a standstill against the iron grid of a gate. The click of her powder-compact told him that houses were in sight.

'You wouldn't think that bit of sun up there could've caught me that quick, would you? And it always goes straight for my nose. It's like a strawberry.'

He waited patiently, picturing the sharp needles of sunlight homing in from every direction on his mother's nose, like bees on ripe fruit. She snapped the compact shut with a sigh. 'There, that'll have to do, I suppose. I only hope there's nobody about, they'll see me coming a mile off.'

'Well you said you wanted to have a nose round the village. And now you've got one, you're complaining.'

'Very funny.'

The handbag dealt out the same treatment to the seat of his jeans as it had to the nettles, then he felt the gate pulled open against his chest. He manoeuvred his way round it and followed her. Three steps led down a bank directly onto the tarmac.

'This is the way we came last night, Matt. It looks like there's only this one road through, right along the coast. If we head to the left through the village a bit, we should come to the driveway up to the cottage. Let's cross over, though, the footpath's on the other side by the houses.'

There were few signs of life, children's voices somewhere in a garden at the back to seaward, a rattle of crockery through an open window, an occasional car, the distant whir of a lawnmower. They followed the street westward. For the first few minutes his mother described the size of the places they were passing, small chalk cottages or larger houses of flint; then she fell silent and devoted her attention to her nose. He could hear the soft clink of her handbag up against her forehead, shielding her face from the light. But he scarcely needed her descriptions. From his right, the rushes told him all he wanted to know, receding to a whisper when a building intervened, then swelling again when it was passed; a constant rising and falling, like the voice of the sea itself. He let it rock him as he walked.

Then, gradually, other sounds became entangled in it, other voices. His grip on his mother's hand tightened.

'Are there people, Mum?'

'There's only a couple of ladies in a front garden up the road. I shouldn't think they'll bite.'

The anxiety of yesterday night rose up in him again, the sound of the rushes changed. A new note stirred in them, a memory of a sharp intake of breath, the swish of a dress against a table, the scuffle of frightened feet. His stomach contracted.

The voices were close now, so close he could touch them. They left their conversation suspended somewhere in the garden, then turned outward to the street, sending greetings and comments on the weather. His mother stopped, answered, spoke of Malham Cottage, introduced him. Behind his smile he waited and listened, straining his ears for any sign of what he dreaded. But no sign came. There was only the sunlight and the voices, warm and welcoming. And it was over, they had moved on. Behind them, the conversation was resumed, picked up again where it had left off.

A vast wave of relief welled up in him and he let go of his mother's hand and slipped his arm through hers, squeezing her to him.

'They didn't notice, Mum, they didn't notice a thing.'

'Oh go on with you. I told you you were a daft idiot.' But her voice was as exultant as his. 'You'd have believed me last night if you'd seen how upset she was when I told her. Poor old Mrs Weaver, I mean.' He hung back for a moment, frowning. 'Now what is it, love?'

He shrugged. 'Oh nothing, I suppose. . . But there is one thing, Mum – I think you *ought* to tell them, like sometimes in London. I'd rather you did, honestly. It'd make it a lot easier for them in the long run, because they wouldn't feel so bad about it afterwards, when they find out. And they're bound to find out, aren't they, if we're going to be here all week?'

The opportunity arose almost at once. The lawnmower which they had heard from a distance stopped its whirrings as they drew level with it and introduced itself as Mr Chapman. Only a moment later, Mrs Chapman had materialised at his side out of nowhere, her voice as elderly as her husband's and betraying the same friendly curiosity about new faces in the village.

After the first few minutes Matthew released his hold on his mother and rested his hands on the low hedge, smiling confidently in the direction of the conversation. His mother's 'posh' voice was back again, and he chuckled inwardly as he pictured her at his side, hiding her fancy shoes behind the hedge and her nose behind her handbag.

He waited for the moment when she would tell them.

When it finally came, its effect was so predictable that he nearly laughed aloud: the Chapmans were just like the people in London. The same startled pause of disbelief, then the same jolliness, the shouting to make sure he could hear them. He grinned to himself, longing for the day when he would be brave enough to give them their answer: 'It's my eyes that are bad, you know, not my ears.' But they meant well enough; they couldn't be expected to understand that his ears were a thousand times better than theirs. He wondered suddenly whether, in all the years they had lived there, they had ever heard the rushes as clearly as he did, or felt the salt on the wind.

His thoughts were interrupted by his mother's voice, speaking with Mr. Chapman. They were discussing the sea.

'It wouldn't hardly be worth it then, you think? With the car, I mean?'

'Not from here it wouldn't. There's only the one track down through the marshes – you probably passed it, just opposite the church. But you couldn't get the car very far down it, and it'd still be a good mile on foot, out along the dyke and over the dunes.'

'Oh well, never mind, we'll manage.'

'Look, if you don't want to do the long trek yourself, why don't you let one of the village lads take him? They'd love it.'

'Oh I couldn't do that!'

'I don't see why not. There's no traffic out there, and he'd be safe as houses with them. They know these parts like the back of their hands.'

With a sudden leap of excitement in his chest, Matthew waited for her answer. But even before it came, he knew what it would be.

'Well, we'll see, but I think we can manage. Anyway, thank you both so much for your kindness. We really must be getting back now. That's the driveway over there, isn't it, up to the cottage?'

'That's the main way. But if you go on a bit further there's another lane up to the left, with a side entrance into the grounds. You can't miss it, and it's a nicer walk – it'll bring you in past the Hall.'

As they moved away the lawnmower struck up again, more loudly than before, Matthew thought, as if it wanted to be sure he could hear it.

'Here's the entrance he was talking about, and about time too. It might be a nicer walk but it must be miles longer this way round. He probably meant it kindly enough, but I'd like to see him try it in these shoes. . . Come on, Matt, what are you doing?'

Matthew remained where he was in the lane, straining his senses back in the direction they had come.

'Mum, are you sure?'

'Sure about what?'

'That we're not being followed.'

'Oh Matt, that's the third time! I've told you we're not.' He heard her limp heavily back to where he was standing and put her handbag up to her forehead. 'I can see for miles. There's not a soul in sight. Come on, if I don't get a cup of tea soon, I'll drop.'

He frowned and turned away, letting her guide him up a shallow bank and into the grounds of the estate. The brightness of the past hour was replaced by dappled greyness, rustling far overhead as if the sky were full of rushes.

'It's a bit cooler for you this way, Mum, with the trees.'

'Not for much longer. I can see the end of them already not far off, with the gardens we saw last night and a bit of the Hall. I hope we're not spotted, that's all, I'd hate them to think we're being nosy or trespassing or something. We'll just have to hope they're not in.'

Somewhere at the back of Matthew's mind, for the first time since their arrival yesterday evening, a memory was jolted half awake. He tried to drag it out from behind the other things which hid it, things which had happened since: the cottage, and Mrs Weaver, and the finding of his path.

'If they *are* about, I suppose I'd better ask if the car woke them up last night. I made enough noise turning round.'

The memory awoke, leaping out from hiding. He pressed his free hand across his eyes to hold it. Lights danced in the blackness, like windows against the night. Last night.

'Here we are, Matt. It's the garden.'

His hand fell away from his face and sunlight rushed across him, gathering itself into sudden shapes of flowers and bushes. Then another shape emerged beyond them, a hazy rectangle capped with chimneys, rising up on steps towards the pillars of an open doorway. He stared unblinking, clenching his teeth to hold the image steady. But it was fading even now, dissolving into empty brightness at the edges. Roofline and garden were lost already. Desperately, he let them go, fixing his eyes on the central point between the pillars, the only point of shadow. Then his heart missed a beat. A figure was taking shape, a deeper darkness in the darkness of the entrance, moving forward, out towards the sunlight, arm raised as it came, waving. In another moment he would see it clearly. Waving, beckoning to him. Joyfully, he began to race towards it.

His mother's hand wrenched him backwards.

'Matt!'

His grip flew free and he crashed down into leaves and gravel. When he looked again, there was only greyness.

'Matt! Are you all right?'

'Yes, I'm OK.'

Her arm was round him, helping him up.

'What were you doing, pulling away like that? And you've skinned your hand. Wait a minute, I've got a hankie somewhere.' She fumbled in her handbag.

'Somebody's seen us, Mum. Haven't they? Somebody in the Hall?'

'Of course nobody's seen us.' He strained his ears as the handkerchief was bound about his knuckles, waiting for footsteps on the gravel. 'There, we'll get some ointment on it when we get home. Come on now, it'll be all right.'

'But somebody *must* have seen us.'

'There's nobody there to see anything, I told you. Now stop worrying.'

'But in the doorway, Mum! Somebody must have seen us from the doorway!'

She ruffled his hair affectionately. 'You *are* an old silly, Matt, worrying about people seeing you. You fell over, that's all. Anybody can fall over, can't they? And anyway, you needn't worry this time. The door's shut. Same as the windows. Everything's boarded up. By the looks of the state of it, the whole place has been boarded up for years.'

Five

Matthew was sitting alone in the long grass by the churchyard wall after lunch, at the end of his pathway, trying to decide whether it had been a successful morning. He decided finally that it hadn't.

They had spent the first half of it shopping. He had suggested they could drive up the coast and find a supermarket, but his mother had insisted on using the village. She'd done enough driving to last her a lifetime, she said, and anyway, you should always use the little shops when you could or they'd go out of business. Then she'd complained all the way home about the price of the butter.

He sighed, scything at the grass with his leg, and reviewed the rest of the morning.

When they had arrived back at the cottage, she had been taken with a baking fit and used up all the butter to make shortbread for tea. Animal shortbread. He had been allowed to cut out the shapes with the usual moulds, which he had been doing for as long as he could remember. Rabbits and ducks. He wondered which worried him more: that she still gave him rabbits and ducks at the age of twelve; or that he still enjoyed being given rabbits and ducks at the age of twelve.

They had had a disagreement about the rabbit, of course. She had said that it must be a rabbit because of the two ears at the top and the bobtail at the bottom, and anyway it had 'Rabbit' printed on the packet when she bought it. He had pointed out that she was looking at it upside down, it was really a man with short freaky legs and a monstrous head with a wart on.

He sighed again and leaned his head back on the edge

of the wall, staring upward into the brightness. It always astonished him that people who had eyes could only ever see things one way round, the way they were told to see them, when it was so obvious that one thing could be two things at the same time if it wanted to. A rabbit could be a man, just as a man could be a rabbit. There were endless possibilities in everything. The question crossed his mind suddenly whether it hadn't been something like that up at the Hall yesterday afternoon, or whether it had just been his eyes playing tricks. With a feeling almost of disappointment he decided that the second explanation was more probable. He considered whether he ought to mention it to his mother but thought better of it: she would only be upset, and anyway, she was hardly likely to want to discuss it. Even the man with the wart had annoyed her.

Somewhere nearby a bee was buzzing, in hungry little rumbles between flowers. And from the churchyard behind him came an answering buzz, like an echo. A lawnmower. He wondered if it was Mr Chapman again. For a moment he remained where he was, screened by the wall. Either he could stay hidden and keep his pathway secret; or he could show himself and enjoy Mr Chapman's surprise at finding him there alone. Finally the surprise won. He stood up.

Almost at once a voice called to him. 'Matthew, isn't it?'

The loud jolliness was unmistakable.

'Yes, Mr Chapman.'

'And you knowing who I am! Well I never! Where's your mum?'

'She's back up at the cottage. I've come for a walk. I often do.'

'Well I'll be. . . You're a wonder, you are!'

'What are you doing?'

'Oh, just having a bit of a mow round the graves, like I do every Monday. I'm through now though. It's a nice little churchyard this is, for a bit of a walk round. Do you want a hand getting over the wall?'

'What?'

Footsteps trod across the grass towards him, and the voice when it came again could have been heard by the dead.

'I said "Do you want a hand getting over the wall?"'

'How do you mean?'

'For your walk. You said you'd come for a walk.'

'Oh. . . Oh yes, thanks.'

A rough, friendly hand took hold of his and he clambered up onto the stone boundary. As his feet touched earth on the farther side a tremor thrilled through him, the same thrill of freedom he had felt when his mother had suggested the pathway, half excitement, half fear, as if he had crossed into forbidden land.

Trying to look as casual as possible, he shuffled his way forward until his foot and arm touched stone; then he propped his back against it cautiously and relaxed with his hands behind him, fingering the engraved lettering. He hoped he was giving a good impression of what his mother called 'drinking up the atmosphere'.

'You're all right now, then, are you?'

'Oh I'm fine, Mr Chapman. Thanks. I'm just going to stay here for a while probably, against this gravestone. Drinking up the atmosphere a bit.'

But Mr Chapman showed little inclination to leave.

'I just can't get over you, I really can't. You knowing that gravestone was there and everything, and only been here a day.'

Matthew gave up any immediate hope of getting back to his pathway and decided to make the best of a bad job.

'Oh it's not that difficult once you get the hang of it. I bet you could do it with your eyes shut with a bit of practice.'

Mr Chapman chuckled. 'I can't even do it with my eyes open sometimes. Gravestones higgledy-piggledy everywhere there are here. I'm always knocking into them when I'm mowing.'

Matthew's heart sank. He clung more firmly to the one gravestone whose position he was sure of, not only feeling out of his depth, but also sorry that he was cheating so much: Mr Chapman was being far more honest than he was.

'Of course, I don't really know my way about the churchyard yet, Mr Chapman, not properly that is. I just have to do it a bit at a time. And I don't know what they *look* like, the gravestones, I mean. I just sort of go by feel. I'd like to know what they look like, really. Can you describe them for me?'

Mr Chapman was silent for a moment and Matthew heard him take off his hat and scratch.

'Well now, as for describing them, that's easier said than done, isn't it? They're not that much to look at really. Just like any other gravestones. As I say, they're higgledy-piggledy, all over the place.'

'But they're not all the same as each other, are they?'

Mr Chapman seemed relieved to be prompted and went on more confidently.

'Oh no, they're not all the same. Some big ones, some little. With different carvings and letterings and everything. Not all the same stone either. Some darker than others, and some marble.'

'Are there any flowers or anything? Does anybody remember?'

'Some flowers there are. More on the newer graves, over on the other side. Not so much up here though, years old some of these are.'

'Whose are they all, Mr Chapman? Are they all for people from Malham?'

'Oh yes, all Malham people they are. Latimers, mainly, up here.'

'Latimers?'

'The family from up at the Hall. Centuries of them there are, laid out here. Grand great family the Latimers were, from what I've heard.'

'You didn't know them, then?'

Mr Chapman chuckled again.

'I might be getting a bit stiff in the joints, but I'm not that old yet. There hasn't been a Latimer up at the Hall in my time.'

'How long has the Hall been empty then?'

'Oh, I don't know. Farther back than I can remember, or anybody else round here for that matter. Near on a hundred years I should reckon. Mrs Weaver might know, next door to you.'

'Mrs Weaver? Why?'

'Her grandmother used to work up at the Hall, so they say. Housekeeper she was, or something of the sort. A lot of servants they had up there in those days.'

'Did Mrs Weaver know the Latimers, then?'

'Good Lord no. Even her mother couldn't have been more than a bit of a girl then, not half as old as you I shouldn't think.'

'Oh.'

'Anyway, I must be getting along. You're sure you're all right now, for finding your way about?'

'Oh I'll be OK, thanks, don't worry. I'll have to get home soon too, or Mum'll start fretting.'

He remained where he was for a while, listening to Mr Chapman making his way round to the north side of the church and trundling the lawnmower through the gate and down the steps they had used yesterday. Its note changed as it crossed the road, smoother and hollower on the tarmac, then it faded to a distant thrum and died away. The sound of the bees took over again.

He wondered how long he had been away from the cottage. He could stay for about an hour, his mother had said, and he doubted whether it had been that long already. But time did funny things when you couldn't see it moving. Perhaps he ought to go, really.

But he was reluctant to leave, to give up the few steps he had taken from the wall to the gravestone. He stroked its rough surface behind him, running his finger along the little valleys that were the lettering. Then a new thought struck him and he turned round and crouched down. He could read it. Without any help from anybody he could read it as easily as his mother read books. He could read it with his fingers. It was just like the plastic alphabet she'd bought him, only the other way round, empty shapes instead of solid ones.

He began in the middle at random, sounding the letters as his fingertips gave them meaning, and even before he had completed his first word he knew what it was. *Latimer.* Just as Mr Chapman had said. He grinned with pride, chasing his fingers higher. The Christian names took shape from the stone. *Rupert Oliver.* Then downwards. *Died August 29th, 1887.* And downwards again, to the final line. He read it and sat back on his heels.

His excitement had gone, replaced by a sudden feeling of regret, catching at his throat and the back of his eyes. For a long moment he stared into space, then he reached out again and laid his fingertips gently on the stone, tracing out the final line once more with a kind of sadness. *Aged 12 years.*

The abruptness of the voice at his side nearly overbalanced him.

'Hello. What are you doing?'

Six

Matthew sprang to his feet and swung round, knowing even as he did so that the movement was too sudden for his balance. In the next instant the ground had slipped from beneath him. He clenched his eyes and waited for its impact. But it didn't come. A hand wrenched him forward and he clung to it, letting the world spin back into place.

'Hey, I'm sorry, I really am. Did I scare you?'

The voice was young, no older than his own, and the note of apology in it was genuine. Matthew released his grip and steadied himself.

'Yes, a bit. I didn't know you were there.'

'Are you sure you're OK?'

'I'm fine now. Thanks for catching me, by the way.'

'That's all right. It was the least I could do, wasn't it? I'd have felt pretty bad if you'd split your head open or something.'

'Yes, so would I, probably.' The laughter which answered his words was infectiously friendly, and he responded to it without hesitation. 'Anyway don't worry, I'm always doing it. It's because of my eyes.'

'Yes I know. You're blind, aren't you.'

Matthew was taken aback. People never used the word to him, they were embarrassed by it. Even his mother avoided it. To hear it used so naturally, with such simple acceptance, filled him with a sense of release.

'Yes. Yes I am.'

When the boy at his side spoke again, the subject seemed already forgotten.

'You're up at the cottage, aren't you?'

'That's right. How did you know?'

'I've seen you around with your mother. This morning and yesterday afternoon.'

A sudden thought crossed Matthew's mind and he blurted it out before he could stop himself.

'You were following us, weren't you?'

But the answer betrayed no hint of surprise or guilt.

'Yes. Right through the village and up the lane.'

'Why?'

'Oh I don't know. Because I'm good at it, I suppose. It's a game I play.'

'That's fantastic. You certainly fooled Mum, anyway. My name's Matt, by the way, Matthew Mason.'

'Yes I know. I'm Roly.'

'Are you here on holiday as well, Roly?'

'No, I live here.'

'It's a great place. I didn't know places like this existed really. I've read about them a bit in books, but it's not the same as being here.'

'How do you read, then?'

'Oh, they're special books, for people who are blind. Braille books, with little dots instead of ordinary letters. You read them with your fingers. I go to a special school back home; they teach you that sort of stuff.'

'Hey, that's amazing. I've never thought of anybody reading things with their fingers. I wish I could.'

'Oh I shouldn't bother, it's pretty slow – the way I do it, it is, anyway. I prefer talking-books, cassettes and things. And Mum reads to me a lot. I like that the best, but I don't ask too much because she's always shattered after work. She never says so but I can always tell. That's why this holiday's so great, it's for her as well as me.'

'Do you go away every year?'

'Well, sort of. But this is the first proper time. It's always been day-trips till now, Southend and places. I really hated them.' The honesty of his own words surprised him. He couldn't remember telling that to anyone before, not even at school. But it seemed easier with Roly somehow; and he was glad to have made the confession, as if it made up a little for his cheating with Mr Chapman. 'I don't think Mum likes it much either, but neither of us ever says anything. It's daft, isn't it?'

'Not really. It'd upset her if you told her, so it's better not to. It's only a few hours, isn't it, and it probably gives her a real kick to take you there. So you're doing it for her as much as she's doing it for you.'

Again, the words startled him by their simplicity. It was as if he had been longing to hear them for years.

'I've never really thought about it like that before.'

'Well, there are always two ways of looking at things, aren't there?'

Matthew grinned. 'Yes,' he said. 'Yes, there are.'

They were silent for a moment, and their silence was echoed back by everything around them, suspending the world in emptiness. It seemed suddenly impossible that Southend could exist at all, or London, or 73 Byron Rise. Perhaps they didn't exist, had never existed, except in his own imagination. The thought made him almost dizzy. He reached out, grateful for the touch of Roly's arm.

'Let's go over and sit on the wall, Roly. It's so quiet here, and it's a really weird feeling not even being able to see things with your ears – if you see what I mean.'

'I can *hear* what you mean, anyway.'

They laughed and made their way back across the few yards to the boundary. The wall was warm to the touch, and its solid roughness comforted him. He clung to it and tipped his head back, letting the grey warmth play on his eyes.

'Have you lived here for long, Roly?'

'Oh yes, always.'

'I'm from London. Have you ever been there?'

'No.'

'It's not really worth the hassle. I can't imagine what it's like to live up here all the time, having the sea so close all the year round and everything. It must be like one great holiday.'

'Yes, I suppose so.'

Matthew brought his head slowly forward again and paused for an instant. There had been a new note in the voice, a note he couldn't quite decipher, like a faint warning-sign. Or a concealment. And he realised suddenly how desperate he was that there shouldn't be any concealment between them. He changed the subject.

'Can you see a pathway behind us?'

'Yes, it's the one up to the cottage. Why?'

'It's my pathway.'

'How do you mean?'

'It's the one I use for getting down here. It's the first real walk I've ever done on my own. It probably sounds a bit daft really, but it was a sort of secret.'

He felt suddenly foolish and turned his head away, wondering whether Roly would laugh. But he didn't. When he finally answered, his voice was unexpectedly gentle.

'Thanks for telling me.'

'Oh that's all right. Hey, what's the time?'

'It must be about threeish, I should think.'

'I can't stay much longer then or Mum'll start panicking, and we're supposed to be having tea in the garden. She'll have a fit, whatever happens, when I tell her I crossed over into the churchyard. I wouldn't have done it if it hadn't been for Mr Chapman. Or at least, if I hadn't shot my mouth off telling him I was some kind of genius at getting around with my eyes shut. Do you know him?'

'Vaguely.'

'He's a really nice bloke. Apart from the way he keeps yelling at me as if I'm some kind of thick idiot. Everybody does it, mind, so I'm used to it now. It's a bit of a laugh really.' Another thought struck him. 'In fact, you're about the first person I've met who doesn't – sighted person, that is. Not that I know many sighted people my age.'

'What was he talking about? Mr Chapman, I mean.'

'About the churchyard mainly. He was sort of describing it for me, like Mum does, the gravestones and everything. He said it was really nice here.'

'It is. I often come here.'

'You can't imagine what it's like after London. It's never quiet at home, not even at night. Living in a flat doesn't help, mind, you can hear the neighbours even when they think they're being quiet. You can even hear them *trying* to be quiet sometimes. It'll be really weird going back to it all after this.' He fell silent, trying to place himself back in Byron Rise, but it was too remote to reach. 'Still, I suppose I'll get used to it again soon enough. It's just that it's so different here, that's all, you can't imagine how peaceful it seems.'

'Yes I can. That's why I like it.'

And again Matthew heard the faint note in the voice beside him which he had caught there a few moments before, but strangely clearer now, though the voice itself had grown quiet. Not a warning note, or concealment. Something else. He sensed the direction of Roly's gaze and let his own drift with it, staring out into greyness.

'Tell me what you can see, Roly. Describe it to me.'

When the voice came again, it was quieter still.

'You know what I can see, you've described it yourself. You can feel it.'

'Tell me what I can feel.'

'Just gravestones, all leaning against the wind. All leaning different ways.' His hand was on Matthew's shoulder suddenly, the other arm outstretched. 'Look, Matt, you can see where they've been leaning against it, its marks are on them.'

And Matthew closed his eyes and saw them. Not as he'd

seen the Hall, not oddly changed and misleading, but as they were now, before him, with their marks of the wind and sea. For an instant he remembered how hard Mr Chapman had tried to describe these same things. In spite of all the old man's words the churchyard had failed to take shape. But now, for no reason that he could understand, it was different. What he felt, and what Roly saw and described, were one and the same.

Suddenly Roly hoisted himself off the wall and stood up. The strangeness of the moment passed.

'What are you doing tomorrow, Matt?'

'Oh, I don't know really. Nothing special, probably.'

'Do you fancy a walk out to the saltmarshes? I'll take you if you like.'

Matthew was stunned, hardly daring to believe what he'd heard.

'Do you mean it? I mean, haven't you got other things on?'

'If I had, I wouldn't suggest it, would I? Say no if you'd rather not. I just thought you might like it.'

'Like it? It'd be great! I just don't want to be a bother, that's all.'

'Some bother. Can you fix it with your mum?'

Matthew tried to make his answer sound as confident as he could.

'Oh I'm sure I can. She's not much of a walker so she'll probably think it's a great idea. Will you come and pick me up?'

Roly paused for a moment. 'Honestly, I'd rather not.'

'Why?'

'Oh I don't know. It's bound to take ages to get started if we do it that way. It'll be much more fun if we just keep ourselves to ourselves.'

Matthew closed his mind to the thought of what his mother would say when he asked to go off with someone she'd never even met. He could worry about that later.

‘Great. We’ll meet here then – we’ll have to, it’s the only place I can get to on my own.’

‘Couldn’t be better. And I tell you what – I’ll teach you my game if you like.’

‘What game?’

‘The one I told you about. We’ll try and get through the whole walk without being spotted.’

‘I couldn’t do that! I can’t see anyone coming!’

‘But you can hear them, can’t you? Your ears are as good as my eyes, better probably. We’ll work as a team. I bet we can do it.’

Matthew felt almost too breathless to answer. The limits of his new freedom made him dizzy, as if his secret pathway seemed suddenly endless.

‘We’ll do it all right.’

‘Great. Two o’clock, then? OK?’

He bit his lip, feeling happier than he’d ever felt in his life. He swung his legs across the wall and looked back with a grateful grin.

‘Thanks, Roly. I’ll be here.’

Then he turned and hurried away.

Seven

Matthew bit the head off a shortbread rabbit and ground it between his teeth. 'I don't see why you're so much against it, that's all.'

'I haven't said I'm against it. I've just said I'm not sure.'

'It comes to the same thing, doesn't it?'

'No it doesn't. I just want to think about it, Matt.'

His mother's deckchair creaked and she rattled awkwardly at the tea-things.

'Look, Mum, there's nothing to think about, is there? It's just a walk. A couple of hours, that's all.'

'But I haven't even met him. I don't know what sort of boy he is, do I?'

'Well his mother hasn't met me either, has she? But I bet she's not making all this fuss.'

'That's different.'

'I don't see why. Anyway, I've told you, he's really nice. He must be, mustn't he, if he wants to lumber himself with me all afternoon.'

'Oh Matt, don't be silly. He ought to think himself lucky to have met you.'

Matthew sighed and closed his eyes. It all seemed so much more difficult now than it had an hour ago, down by the churchyard wall. He chewed his way through the rest of the rabbit with a growing feeling of misery. He *had* to meet Roly tomorrow, and go on the walk. In all his life he couldn't remember wanting anything more desperately.

'I really want to go, Mum, more than anything.'

'I know, Matt, I know you do. But you've got to see it from my side as well. I don't know anything about this boy, he could be anybody. What sort of family does he come from?'

Matthew hesitated, annoyed with himself for not having found out. It was the sort of question his mother was bound to ask.

'How do you mean?'

'Well, what do his parents do?'

'I don't know, I didn't bother to ask. I don't see what's so important about that.'

'Of course it's important. Does he sound as if he comes from a nice background?'

'How am I supposed to know?'

'Well you must be able to tell by the way he talks, surely? Does he sound rough?'

'Oh Mum, what difference does it make? And he doesn't, anyway.'

'Whereabouts does he live? . . . Well, didn't you find out?'

Matthew felt suddenly angry with himself and with her.

'No, I didn't. I should've taken his fingerprints, I suppose, but I forgot. Look, Mum, it's only a walk!'

'That's all very well, but what if anything happens? What am I supposed to do then?'

'Nothing's *going* to happen though, is it? I shouldn't think there are savages or wild elephants or anything.'

'That's daft. You know what I mean.'

'No I don't.'

'It'd be different if I could get to know him a bit first, that's all.'

There was a long silence. Somewhere down on the main road a car was attempting to start, whirring up and then choking away into silence. Matthew listened to it idly, sympathising with its helplessness. Then his mother sat forward with unexpected briskness and put her cup on the garden table. He wondered what was coming.

'Wait a sec, Matt, I've had an idea. I don't know why we didn't think of it before.' He turned his face towards her with a sense of tension, half hope, half foreboding. 'Listen, I could come with you. I'd like a bit of a walk round the saltmarshes. We could all go together and take a picnic.'

His stomach sank. Of all possible difficulties this was the one he had least foreseen, and he felt suddenly more wretched than ever. He hated the thought of having her with him tomorrow, and hated himself for hating it. As he sat there speechless, he could almost hear her enthusiastic smile fading.

'Well, what do you think, love? You don't look very keen. It'd be fun, wouldn't it?'

'I suppose so. It's just not what we'd planned, that's all. We'd planned to go on our own.'

The deckchair creaked again as she sat back.

'I see. I suppose you don't want him to meet me? Is that it?'

It was hopeless. He remained where he was, without answering. There seemed no answer he could give. His resentment drained away, and he felt suddenly sorry for her. He understood her feelings; she wasn't being awkward, she was just puzzled and hurt. He wondered if he could ever make her understand his own feelings.

'Listen, Mum, it's not like that, you know it's not. And it's only for a couple of hours. It'll probably only be tomorrow, he'll probably get tired of it after that. And even if he doesn't, it can't be more than four days, can it? We've only got till Saturday morning.'

It was the first time he had made the calculation and it filled him with a new sense of wretchedness. He hadn't realised the time was so short. He got up and made his way to the edge of the garden, supporting himself on the hedge and staring emptily seaward. The car had started up now and was moving freely along the main road. He envied it its success. Then his attention sharpened. The tyres had changed their note from tarmac to gravel, and there was a faint squawking of branches on glass. Somebody was coming up the drive.

He followed its approach, remembering their own journey on Saturday; a gear-change at the fork, and a smoother run up the final few yards into the open. He was surprised to hear it draw up before the cottage even though he knew there was nothing beyond. A door opened and shut, then footsteps came towards him through the grass. He acknowledged them with a sudden smile, grateful for an intrusion he thought he recognised. The loudness of the voice confirmed it.

'Hello, Matthew, I don't suppose I need to tell you who I am, do I? Hello, Mrs Mason.'

His mother was behind him now, with her hand on his shoulder.

'Oh hello, Mr Chapman. I was wondering who it could be, using the driveway.'

He answered her unexpressed question.

'I've just brought a few groceries and things up for Mrs Weaver. I usually pop up in the week. She can't get around much now, down to the village and the like.'

'Oh no, I should've thought! I could've done a bit of shopping for her this morning, and asked her round to a cup of tea or something!'

'Don't you worry yourself, it's easier when you know her needs. But I'm sure she'd be glad of a cup of tea some time, she likes a bit of company, does Mrs Weaver.' The voice rose again. 'Well, Matthew, did you have a nice walk?'

'Yes thanks, Mr Chapman, it was great.'

'How far did you get?'

'Oh, only to the churchyard.'

'And what's the next big excursion?'

Matthew bit his lip and stared at the ground. In the awkward silence which followed he felt the hand on his shoulder tighten. When Mr Chapman's voice came again, it sounded suddenly embarrassed, with an attempt at a chuckle.

'Sorry, Mrs Mason, have I said something? I'm always

putting my big foot where it's not wanted.'

His mother rallied.

'No of course you haven't, Mr Chapman. It was just funny, that's all, you asking. Matthew and me were only just having a little chat about it when you dropped by. He's met a boy from the village, you see, who's offered to take him out tomorrow, over on the saltmarshes.'

'There, what did I tell you? A nice crowd of lads they are round here, he'll be safe enough with any of them. And it'll spare your legs a bit, too.'

'Well, actually I was thinking I might go with them perhaps.'

'You could, of course, it's not a bad little trek if the weather's all right.' He chuckled again. 'But they'll probably enjoy the chance of getting off on their own a bit. No offence meant, mind, but you know how it is. I always used to, I can tell you.'

Matthew could have hugged him. He heard his mother's hesitation behind him, and held his breath.

'I think I ought to meet the boy first though, Mr Chapman. I mean, I don't know anything about him.'

'Who is it, Matthew?'

'Somebody called Roly.'

'Roly? Oh, Roland Johnson that'll be, he's the only Roland round here. Nice family the Johnsons are, what I know of them. Big house at the other end of the village – father's in business of some sort over in Wells, I think. He'll be all right with Roland, Mrs Mason, don't you worry. The lad's been here all his life from what I remember, so he should know his way round the creeks by now.'

'Oh, I see.'

Matthew raised his head and looked towards Mr Chapman, grinning helplessly. It was over, he was sure it was. Even though his mother said no more, he could sense that the barrier had been crossed. Tomorrow afternoon rose up again before him, as free and simple as it had seemed down by the churchyard wall. But his surge of relief was short-lived. Mr Chapman's next words struck him like a blow in the stomach.

'I'll be getting along now, then. If you've got a spare minute, Matthew, I could use another pair of hands. There are a couple of boxes in the car.'

'How do you mean?'

'Groceries, like I said, for Mrs Weaver. Have you been round to see her yet?'

'No.'

'Well, it'll be as good a chance as any. And you can ask her that question about how long the Hall's been empty. She'd be really pleased to see you, I know.' Matthew swung his head and stared in blank desperation at his mother, but Mr Chapman answered for her. 'Oh I'm sure your mum won't mind you being away for a bit, will you, Mrs Mason?'

He felt an encouraging squeeze on his shoulder as his mother replied.

'Of course I won't mind. – You go on, Matt, and give Mr Chapman a bit of a hand. He's right, she will be pleased, you'll see.'

Dumbly, he let himself be guided over to the car and felt the weight of cardboard in his arms, filling his nostrils with a smell of soap and detergent. As they moved away again, shoulder to shoulder, he could sense his mother's eyes watching him from the garden and turned his head towards her again, wondering what expression was on her face. Then Mr Chapman's voice came from beside him, calling in the same direction.

'Don't worry, Mrs Mason, he'll be all right for getting back. Mrs Weaver'll watch him round if I've gone.'

The final words took his breath away.

'You're not going, Mr Chapman, are you?'

'I am in a minute. You don't mind staying on a bit, do you?

There's bound to be a cup of tea at the ready, and old people like a chat, especially with you young folk.'

'But she might be busy or something.'

'I doubt it. And she'll stop whatever she's doing, if she is. It'll be a real treat for her to see a new face.'

They were almost there; the same grass he had heard his mother crossing two nights before, the same doorbell, the same muffled radio swooping into silence, the same footsteps approaching through the hallway. With his hands clutching at the box, he waited for the door to open.

Eight

In the little back-kitchen Matthew stood by the boxes on the table, too numb even to remember how he'd got there. He listened. The voices were saying goodbye to each other at the front door, Mr Chapman was leaving already. Then the door clicked shut, closing him inside the house.

An icy, high-pitched whine shrilled up his back and into his ears. He thought for a moment that he was going to be sick. The footsteps were coming back, limping slowly out of the hall and into the sitting-room. They stopped in the kitchen doorway. He pressed his back to the table and held his breath, waiting.

'Oh my dear.'

The voice seemed to come from an endless distance, so changed and saddened that he scarcely recognised it. Its helplessness stunned him. Without any warning, from somewhere deep inside him, a flood of pity and relief welled up. He tried to smile, tried to speak, to tell her it was all right. But no sound came. Somewhere in the stillness a clock was ticking.

'My dear, I'm so sorry.'

The sadness of the voice was everywhere, filling the silence and the room and him himself. He felt it in his chest and at the back of his eyes, begging for release.

Smiling at last, he let it have its way.

'Are you sure you can't manage another cup of tea before it gets cold?'

'Honestly I can't, Mrs Weaver, I had two round at home before I came.'

'Well you can finish off the biscuits at least, there's one left on the plate just asking to be eaten.'

With a grin he fumbled at the coffee-table and then sat back in his armchair again, listening to the old hands opposite him trembling at the lid of the teapot. She poured herself another cup and sipped at it gratefully. Mr Chapman had been right, she was glad he had come.

Then he stopped chewing suddenly and sat motionless. Her voice came immediately, confirming his suspicion.

'What's the matter, dear?'

'Oh nothing. . . That is, I just thought you were looking at me.'

'I was. How did you know?'

'I always do, I can sort of sense it.'

'You don't mind, do you?'

'No, not usually. It's just that. . .'

He bit his tongue and paused, at a loss how to go on.

'I know, Matthew, I know. It's because of the other night, isn't it?'

'Yes.'

She didn't answer at once. He could hear her struggling within herself to find the right words.

'Matthew, listen. I'd so like to forget about it. It was just silly of me. And when I found out afterwards, from your mother. . . Well, I've been so upset about what you must have thought. You don't know how upset I've been. I didn't know, Matthew, really I didn't. How could I have known?'

'What was it then, Mrs Weaver? What made you jump like that?'

She paused again, stirring her tea round and round in the cup. Then she put down the spoon in the saucer.

'I got in a muddle, that's all. Old people get silly notions sometimes, you'll know that yourself one day perhaps. Now let's try and forget it, shall we, I'd so much like to – and that'll be the best way of showing me I'm forgiven.'

And they forgot it. They talked of other things, London

and cassettes, the school for the blind and his teachers, his doctor and the operations he had had, and how he read books with his fingers. He told her what it was like not being able to see and she told him what it was like not being able to walk, and they laughed at themselves and each other, comparing their bruises. Then he explained how his mother had found the advertisement for the cottage, and slowly London receded from their talk and Malham took over.

'It must be great to live here. I wish I could.'

'Yes, I don't think I could have asked for anything better. But then, I can't really compare. This is the only place I've known.'

'Have you always lived here, in this cottage?'

'Always.'

'On your own?'

'Bless you, no. There was a Mr Weaver too, you know. But he died a long time ago, in the last war.'

'What was he like?'

'Oh, he was a fine-looking man. You can see for yourself – there's a photo on. . .'

He heard her catch her breath and fall silent, and grinned across at her.

'It's all right, Mrs Weaver, really it is. – Honestly, it doesn't worry me when people say things like that, it only worries me when they get all embarrassed about it. Mum never bothers what she says any more, and that's nice.'

'Oh Matthew, what can I say?'

'Don't say anything, I told you. When you come to think about it, it was a real compliment, wasn't it? It's like me asking you whether you'd fancy coming for a run round the saltmarshes tomorrow.'

She laughed. 'You ought to be careful, I might take you up on it. *Are* you going out there tomorrow?'

He remembered again, and the thought thrilled through him.

'Yes. With a boy from the village. We're going on our own – so long as I can clear it with Mum, that is. But I think it'll be OK.'

'Which boy is it?'

'Roland Johnson. He's from the big house at the other end of the village, Mr Chapman says.'

'Oh, you'll be all right with Roland, I'm sure. I knew him when he was born. You tell your mother she needn't worry.'

'Great, I'll do that. Do you know the Johnsons well?'

'I did. Not now though. I shouldn't think I've seen Roland for a couple of years or more. It's out of the way, up here, for visits.'

'Do you own all this land, Mrs Weaver? . . . Why are you laughing?'

'The thought of it! Matthew, of course I don't! I don't even own this cottage.'

'What?'

'I just rent it.'

'But you're not on holiday, you live here.'

'As if that makes any difference! Where do you think I could find enough money to buy something like this?'

'Oh I see. You mean it's like our place in London, a sort of council place?' He wondered suddenly if he should have told her; his mother was funny about things like that. But her voice showed no hint of surprise.

'Yes, very much like that. The only difference is that it's not owned by the council but by a private family. The Latimers still own it.'

'But I thought they'd gone, ages ago? The Hall's empty, isn't it?'

'Oh yes, they're not here now. The Hall's been empty for years, a hundred years it must be since the last Latimers lived here. But they still own it just the same, cottages, grounds, everything. I keep my eye on the cottage next door and clean up a bit between visits; and the grounds are mowed now and then by a sort of contract firm of gardeners. It's all handled by agents or solicitors or something of the kind. The Latimers never come back now themselves.'

'Why not?'

'Oh, times have changed, I suppose. It was different in the old days, you wouldn't believe the stories my grandmother used to tell. She was the housekeeper up at the Hall, you see – that's how we came to be in the cottage in the first place. The dances they used to have up there, and the parties, with carriages rolling up the drive and the ladies all in silk dresses and the gentlemen in tailcoats. Champagne used to flow like water up at the Hall, she said. They were grand and wealthy all right, the Latimers were, and generous with it too. But it's different now, people run things differently. They get agents to manage things for them.'

'Where are they now, then? The Latimers, I mean.'

'Oh, somewhere abroad. Very, very distant cousins of the original family. I shouldn't think their names are even Latimer any more.'

'Why doesn't the original family still own it?'

For an instant Matthew thought he caught a hesitation in her voice. She was speaking again before he could be sure.

'Oh, there wasn't anyone left to inherit it directly, not from that branch of the family.'

'How do you mean?'

'Well, when the Latimers finally went away, a hundred years ago, there weren't any sons and daughters to take it all over. So it went to cousins, and cousins of cousins. That sort of thing.'

'Why don't all these cousins and people come back and live here then, in the Hall, I mean?'

'Oh Matthew, it's not fit to live in now! It's derelict. They might have saved it fifty years ago if they'd wanted to, but they didn't. And it's past saving now. It'd cost a fortune to do up a place that size, and another fortune to live there. Can you imagine what the heating would cost, apart from anything else?'

'But why was it empty in the first place? I mean, why did the Latimers leave it a hundred years ago?'

His attention sharpened suddenly. It was there again, but more distinct this time, the same hesitation in the voice.

'They didn't want to live there any more, I suppose.'

'But why, when they'd been there so long? Why did they all suddenly leave?'

'Oh it wasn't as dramatic as all that! You make it sound as if there were hundreds of them, all leaving at once. There were only the two of them eventually, only the parents.'

'Parents? Whose parents?'

The pause came again, but so long this time that it startled him. He strained his ears, trying to catch its meaning, wondering if it would ever end. Then she began to lift her cup towards the table beside her, and her voice returned, unnaturally loud.

'Oh Matthew, such a lot of questions to an old woman! You seem to forget that I wasn't even born then! Anything I know I only know from my grandmother or my mother – and even my mother was only a little girl of six when it happened.'

'When what happened?'

The cup hit the table with a clatter and rolled in its saucer.

'Oh you know what I mean – when the Latimers left. Now stop teasing my old brains with questions about a hundred years ago.'

She changed the subject so quickly that he was no longer sure himself whether it was because there was nothing more to tell or because there was something more which couldn't be told. But whichever it was, he felt, there was no way in which he could pursue it. And so he let it slip away.

When the clock chimed six, he stood up to leave.

'I must go now, Mrs Weaver, Mum'll be wondering where

I've got to. I'd just. . .' His voice sounded suddenly awkward and he bit his lip. 'Well, I'd just like to say I'm sort of glad I came round.' Feeling foolish even as he did it, he held out his hand. But she accepted it gently.

'So am I, Matthew.'

'And . . . well, perhaps I might drop in again some time, before we leave, I mean.'

'I'd like that.'

'And you never know, we might be back next year. I'm not saying we will, mind, because I haven't mentioned it to Mum. But I'd really like to. And I can come and see you again.'

The hand stirred slightly in his and fell away. There was a pause which he couldn't understand.

'That would be nice, my dear. But I'm afraid it won't be possible.'

'Why not?'

'Because I'm going away. By this time next year, I'll be gone.'

A pang of alarm shot through him, not only for Mrs Weaver but for himself too, as if something he had been counting on more than anything else in the world, something which he hadn't even expressed to himself in words, were about to be taken from him.

'But where are you going to?'

'Oh, it's a nice place, they say, down in Norwich, a place for old people. Don't worry, I've planned it for a long time now, to be ready for the day when I'm too old to see to myself any more. It's just come a bit sooner than I thought, that's all.'

'What has?'

'The sale, or the planning permission, or whatever they call it.'

'I don't understand.'

'It's all going, Matthew. The cottages are being sold, and

they're building on the estate. Bungalows and things, so I've heard. And the Hall's to be pulled down, to make way.'

'No! They can't!'

A strange panic seized him and he reached out for her arm and clung to it, as if to stop her moving away.

'Oh my dear, you mustn't be so upset! I wouldn't ever have told you if I'd thought you'd take it like this. Please, don't. Don't let our visit together finish the way it began. And think how *I* must feel, after all these years.'

He forced out an answer through the tightness in his throat.

'I'm sorry, Mrs Weaver, I really am.'

'Well, there it is. Times change, as I said, and we must just accept them. We can't hold on to things for ever, can we?'

'No, I suppose not.'

'Let them go, Matthew, when you have to. And until then, enjoy them. Four days are a long time, my dear.'

'Yes.'

She led him out through the hallway and opened the front door.

'Now you go and have a nice evening with your mum – and remember both your promises, won't you?'

He looked towards her questioningly.

'Which promises, Mrs Weaver?'

'To come and see me again before you go. And until then, to enjoy yourself. It's the saltmarshes tomorrow, isn't it?'

'Yes. Yes it is.'

'Run along then. You just think about tomorrow and forget about the rest.'

And he ran, sure-footed across the grass, waving goodbye as he went.

Nine

Matthew hurried along the final few yards of the pathway and threw himself down in the shelter of the wall. He paused for a moment, breathless, hardly daring even to whisper the question he had waited so long to ask. The morning had seemed endless.

'Roly, are you there?'

Then he let his head drop back against the stonework, closing his eyes and grinning with relief. The familiar voice had answered, whispering from beyond the wall.

'Of course I'm here, idiot. Come on over, the coast's clear.'

A hand reached out to help him and he clambered across the boundary and fell in a heap on the other side.

'It's great of you to come, Roly. Thanks.'

'Save your breath, you'll need it. There's nobody round the church and the track down to the creeks isn't used much by anybody. But the street's going to be tricky – listen.'

Matthew took a deep breath to control his panting, and strained his ears outward. The churchyard itself was shimmering with the murmur of insects, and from far beyond the north wall came an answering murmur, like an echo, where the rushes waited. But between the two a barrier of sharper sounds rose up.

'It's busier than it was yesterday, Roly, isn't it? It's probably because of the jumble-sale. It starts about now.'

'Yes I know.'

'Mum heard this morning in the village. She's going along in a bit. Still, it'll take her mind off me.'

'Wasn't she too keen on the idea?'

'You can say that again. Anyway, so long as I'm back in one piece by about four it'll be OK.'

'Let's get going then, that only gives us a couple of hours. Keep crouched down so as we won't be spotted from the road.'

He took Matthew's sleeve and steered him through the clutter of gravestones, following the same direction as on Sunday afternoon. The memory of his mother's slow progress against the nettles made Matthew uneasy and he resisted Roly's swift guidance at first, flinching at every step and bracing himself for collision. But no collision came. Even before they had reached the gateway he had relaxed, surrendering himself totally to the hand on his arm.

'Get down!'

Matthew ducked and felt Roly squatting at his side. The noises of the street were close now, separated from them by the thickness of stone.

'Wait here a sec, Matt. I'm going to spy out the land through the gateway.'

Matthew heard him crawl a few feet through the long grass to the right and pause. From the far end of the village a lorry loomed up, shook the ground threateningly as it drew level, then receded to a distant rumble. Voices and laughter took its place, and the squeak of pram-wheels on the opposite pavement. The grasses swished again at his side and Roly was back, his words barely a whisper.

'It's almost clear. Just the Carters with Mrs Edwards heading left. Once they're past, we're going to make a break for it. Come on, but keep low.'

On hands and knees he followed Roly along by the wall and heard him easing the gate open. The footsteps grew louder and he held his breath, praying that his heartbeat wouldn't give him away. When Roly's voice feathered against his ear, he nearly cried out.

'OK, forty-five seconds. Three steps down, across the road, and the track's dead opposite. It's rough tarmac for about a hundred yards, and sharp left for another hundred or so. Then we're on the footpath out through the rushes. Be prepared for me to put the brakes on any time once we reach it. OK?'

'OK.'

'And Matt – don't try and slow us down whatever you do. I won't let you hurt yourself, I promise. You can trust me, can't you?'

'Yes.'

'Right then. On the word, just let yourself go and run like the wind. Five seconds . . . Now!'

And Matthew let himself go, and ran. The wind took him, lifting him across the tarmac, into the track and on, until he didn't know any longer whether it was the wind he could hear, or the rushes, or his own breathing. He threw his head back, staring giddily upward into emptiness and moving faster than he'd ever moved before, with the hand on his sleeve guiding him like eyes. Then they were tumbling together into grass, breathless with laughter, as the world spun down.

'We made it, Matt! I told you we would! They didn't even look round!'

Matthew remained where he was on his back, grinning behind closed eyes. His legs were still running, even though he knew they had stopped, propelling him irresistibly on. They must be flying him upward now, into space. He flung his arms wide in the grass.

'Hey, are you OK, Matt?'

'OK?' He propped himself up, with the ground solid and spiky against the palms of his hands. 'I don't think I've ever felt so great, ever. I can't describe it. It's like being set free or something.'

'Yes. I suppose it must be.'

Matthew turned his head sharply in the direction of the voice at his side. For the first time that afternoon, it had been there again in Roly's answer, he was sure, the same strange, quiet note he had heard yesterday. He listened to its echo in the air, wondering. But the wind blew it from him and Roly spoke again, as bright and eager as before.

'And there's more to come, Matt. You wait till we get to the creeks!'

For twenty minutes they made their way along the narrow footpath through the rushes. The murmurings which Matthew had heard from far off, from the cottage and the churchyard, enveloped him now, stretching away on either side to the edge of hearing. There was no other sound anywhere.

'It's so empty, Roly! Like the sea. It's like walking through the sea.' The happiness he felt was almost painful. 'I *wish* I could see it, more than anything in the world. Describe it to me, Roly. Like you did yesterday. Then I'll know what it's like as clear as if I could really see it.' He stopped speaking as abruptly as he had started and bit his lip, convinced that Roly would laugh. The suggestion had sounded idiotic.

But he didn't. He showed no sign of surprise. With his hand on Matthew's shoulder he steered him gently round and pointed outward, speaking close by his ear. His voice was hardly louder than the rushes, but there was excitement in it too, and pleasure.

'Perhaps we *are* walking through the sea, Matt. Look! Close your eyes and look! Can you see them over there against the sky? Masts, dozens of them, and so clear!'

'Is it the creeks, Roly? Are there boats moored on the creeks?'

'They might be moored. Or they might be sailing. It's hard to tell from here, isn't it? They might be sailing towards us on the rushes.'

And Matthew smiled and saw them, masts against the sky, swaying on a sea of rushes. Then he broke away, pulling Roly with him.

'Come on, Roly, I'll race you to them!'

Roly laughed. 'Go on then, I'm holding on to you! The

path's as straight as an arrow. I'll tell you when to stop!'

In less than five minutes Matthew heard the swishings against his legs fall suddenly silent, as if his footsteps had swept them aside. As the footpath widened out and gave way to rough tarmac again, Roly put the brakes on from behind.

'Hold it, or you'll be up to your neck.'

'Are we there, Roly? Is it the creeks? Are the boats here? Is it the masts we saw?'

'Yes. They're all stranded in mud, waiting for the tide to turn. Listen!'

Matthew let the drumming of the pulsebeat in his ears die away, and then caught his breath. There was a sound in the air, everywhere, but so faint and strange that he could hardly catch it. Then the rushes stirred and the sound rose again above them, like silver. He touched Roly's arm and spoke in a whisper.

'What is it?'

'Look at the boats, Matt. Listen, and tell me.'

'It's the masts, isn't it? The lines blowing against the masts!'

'Listen to them.'

The wind stirred again, and the lines tinkled with it.

'They're like music.'

'They *are* music, Matt. It's the music of the creeks.'

They sat down together in the rough grass at the edge of the tarmac, with the rushes at their backs, and listened for a while in silence as the sounds rose and fell on the wind. The mud of the creeks was sharp with the smell of salt, like a promise of the sea. Matthew lay back and closed his eyes, letting himself float and drift on the emptiness of it all.

'It's incredible, Roly. I've never heard anything like it, ever. It's like being at the end of the world.'

'No, not yet. A bit farther yet. Out beyond the dunes, that's where it really ends.'

'The sea?'

'Yes.'

'How far is it?'

'A mile perhaps, out along the dyke through the saltings.'

'Too far?'

'Too far for today.' Matthew felt the words tingle through him and held his breath, not daring to speak his next question. As if he had caught its silent echo, Roly answered it. 'Yes, tomorrow would be best. Would you like to?'

'*Like* to! I'd like it more than anything!'

'Great. Try and get yourself an extra hour – it'll be worth it, I promise.'

Matthew closed his eyes again and felt a wave of happiness surge up inside him and sweep him outward through the rushes.

'Where do the rushes end, Roly?'

'They don't. You can't see them any more once you've crossed the dunes, but they're still there. You can hear their voices, out in the sea. They go on for ever.' Matthew heard him roll over onto his stomach and prop his chin in his hands. 'It's said that if you whisper a secret to them they'll never forget it. And if you came here again a hundred years from now and listened, they'd whisper it back to you. Why don't you try it? Any secret'll do.'

Matthew grinned. 'No thanks. I'm not that daft.'

'What's daft about it? Don't you believe it?'

'It doesn't make much difference whether I do or not, does it? I mean, it's a pretty safe story. It's not ever likely to be proved, is it?'

'Why not?'

'Well I'm not exactly likely to be able to get back here in a hundred years to find out, am I?'

Roly was silent for a moment, then he sat up.

'Mind you,' he said, 'there are always two ways of looking at things, remember?'

'How do you mean?'

'Well, why don't you try listening instead?'

'What for?'

'You might hear something.'

'Such as?'

'Your secret.'

'But I'd only hear that if I'd whispered it a hundred years ago, idiot.'

'Exactly. So try listening. Like I said, you might hear something.'

Matthew frowned, confused by the idea. Then its strange logic dawned on him and he scrambled uneasily to his feet, away from the rushes. Roly joined him, chuckling.

'There! Typical, of course! First you want proof, then when it's handed you on a plate you're too scared to try it.'

'Why don't *you* have a go, then?'

'No thanks.'

'Why not?'

'Too scared.'

Matthew laughed, then his face became serious again.

'So you *do* believe it, Roly?'

'Believe what?'

'That we might hear something. That people might be able to sort of come back.'

'Of course. Don't you?' But before Matthew had time to answer, Roly had taken his arm. 'Oh come on, let's forget it. I want to show you the boats.'

They wandered on down as close as they could to the creek where the ground grew wetter. There they stopped for a time, while Roly described the boats and Matthew saw what he described, closing his eyes against the wind. Then they climbed upward again to the rough tarmac track and Matthew paused reluctantly, knowing that he would have to leave.

'I suppose we ought to be going, Roly, it must be past three already.' The sound of his own words pained him, as if they were announcing the end of his freedom. Then another thought comforted him. 'If I get back on time today, I bet Mum'll be OK about tomorrow.'

'Fine, we'll just walk down to the end of the creek then, and head back after that.'

'How far is it?'

'Only about a couple of hundred yards. The tarmac finishes then, and the dyke starts. We'll run it if you want – you know, like earlier on. There's nothing in the way.'

Matthew paused, breathless with a sudden idea.

'Roly, do you think I could run it on my own? Is it wide enough to be safe?'

'Plenty, I'd have thought. And there's grass and rushes on one side and mud on the other, so you'll soon know if you go off course.' Then he laughed. 'I'd better go to the other end though, and yell stop, or you'll be up on the dyke and off to the sea today. I'll give you a shout when I'm ready.'

With a tremble of excitement Matthew heard him turn and set off, his footsteps receding into the wind. Then his voice sprang out of the distance and echoed along the creek.

'Can you hear me, Matt?'

'Yes!'

'Can you sense where I am?'

'Yes!'

'OK, it's all yours!'

And Matthew leapt forward with the ground flying behind him, running more freely than he had ever run before. The air caught him and flung him on faster, until his legs seemed to have life of their own and he let them take him, laughing into the endless greyness. Then, without warning, the greyness shifted. It wasn't inside his eyes any more, it was outside them, as if he could see it before him. In sudden alarm he tried to stop himself but his feet drove him on towards it. It blew against him like mist from the sea, dissolving around him as he ran. And as it cleared, his eyes seemed to open on what lay beyond, not daylight, but darkness, and the dyke rising up against the night. A figure was taking shape from the shadows at the end of the track, where Roly would be waiting. But it wasn't waiting, it was moving away from him up the side of the dyke and seaward. Desperation seized him and he threw himself on faster, begging it over and over again to stop. Then the mists were returning and the calling growing fainter, as if his cries were only echoes.

Stop!!

The voice yelled out again and he collided with it and fell backwards. For a second he was suspended, then the ground met him and he lay sprawled in grass. Roly was close beside him.

'Matt, didn't you hear me, for God's sake? I couldn't have yelled much louder! – Are you OK?'

Matthew sat up, panting.

'What happened, Roly?'

'You tell me!'

'Did I crash into you?'

'Very funny. – Why on earth didn't you stop when I told you?'

'I don't know. I didn't think it was you shouting. I sort of thought it was me. . .'

'What's that supposed to mean? I was standing here screaming like a lunatic.'

'All the time?'

'What?'

'Were you standing here all the time, waiting?'

'Well of course I was! Where else am I supposed to have been?'

'I just thought you weren't here any more, that's all. I thought you were running away.'

In the silence which followed his words, Matthew sensed Roly's startled gaze and felt suddenly foolish. He took a deep breath.

'Oh I'm sorry, Roly, really I am. It was because of the racing about or something, I expect. I'm not used to it, that's all. It was daft to have done it.'

'Oh well, forget it. So long as you're OK, that's the main thing. Come on, give me your hand and I'll haul you up. . . Now, are you sure there aren't any bones broken or anything?'

'Yes. Are my jeans mucked up?'

'Well, the grass-marks show a bit but they're OK apart from that.'

'Not bad enough for Mum to go crazy?'

'No, don't worry. But she'll go crazy if we don't get a move on.'

Following Roly, he made his way back along the tarmac towards the footpath and it was only when he reached it that he paused and turned seaward again. He screwed up his eyes, as if trying to see. But there was nothing but the grey salt-wind.

'Come on, Matt!'

Shrugging his shoulders, he hurried after Roly through the rushes.

Ten

The sea must be near now. He could taste it on his lips.

He yelled back against the wind. 'Can you see the salt, Roly?'

'What?'

'The salt! The air must be full of it, like snow. Can you see it like I can feel it?'

'Only when I shut my eyes. Go on, keep moving. I've got hold of you. We'll be there in twenty minutes.'

In single file they pressed forward again along the narrow track high on the dyke with Roly guiding from behind, as he had guided yesterday, his hands on Matthew's shoulders. Wind was everywhere, deafening their ears and engulfing the creeks and rushes below them in a tide of sound. They stopped for a moment as the dyke curved seaward, listening.

'Are you sure it's not the sea, Roly? Down below us, I mean?'

'It's only the rushes. They're telling us about it, that's all. Not long now and we'll see for ourselves – we'll be off the dyke soon and down into the saltings.' He turned Matthew's shoulders slightly and spoke close by his ear. 'Look, you can see the dunes already, out there in the sky.'

Matthew closed his eyes and smiled. 'They're like clouds, aren't they?'

'Just like clouds, only softer. Have you ever walked up clouds before?'

'No.'

'Come on then, I challenge you.'

They moved on, twisting and turning with the path. Then the dyke began to tail away and they stumbled downward onto flat earth.

'The wind's gone, Roly!'

'No it hasn't, it's still up there. We've given it the slip, that's all. Let's get a move on before it spots us – we can go faster for a bit, it's as wide and empty as anything. We're in the real saltings now.'

'Why are they called saltings?'

'Just keep licking your lips and stop asking questions.'

They were side by side again now, hurrying across what seemed like an endless wasteland, damp underfoot as if the sea had touched it.

'Why's it so wet, Roly?'

'Why do you think? Because we're walking on the bottom of the sea, that's why.'

'Are you joking?'

'Of course I'm not. When the tide's in full, this is nothing but water. The sea comes sweeping in past the dunes and up the creeks, filling everything. Why else do you think the boats were there yesterday?'

Matthew bent his head back, staring up into the void. High above him the wind was rushing in to the land, like a tide. He shivered suddenly and felt Roly turn towards him and pause.

'It's OK, Matt, don't worry. The sea's way out at the moment, it won't be turning for ages.'

'But what if it does?'

'It won't. I told you.'

'But how do you know?'

'I just know. I've lived here all my life, haven't I? I've been down here by the sea every day for as long as I can remember. Just sitting and watching. I know its ways now.' And faintly, for the first time since yesterday afternoon, Matthew thought he could hear in the voice at his side the same puzzling note. But it had passed again almost before he could be sure. 'Anyway, we'll be up on the dunes soon, and the sea never touches *them*.'

'Why not?'

'They're too high for it. Like clouds – remember?'

As the ground began to rise again, Matthew believed him. The damp sea-bed disappeared and gave way to a soft cushion of dryness, shallow at first and gentle to walk on, then deepening as it rose higher, pulling his feet downward. He could feel it, grainy between his toes, dragging at his trainers and sifting away behind them. He laughed as Roly hauled at his arm.

'Come on, Matt. What's so funny?'

'I've just found out what clouds are made of, that's all.'

'What then?'

'Salt. Mountains of the stuff.'

With a chuckle Roly let go of his hand suddenly and he felt himself staggering backwards and landing on the seat of his jeans, pillowed in sand.

'You just hang on there for a sec. I'm going to the top.'

'What for?'

'To spy out the land on the other side. We don't want to spoil our record by getting spotted now.'

'How far is it?'

'Only a few yards. Don't eat all the salt before I get back.'

Matthew heard him clamber a few steps higher and felt the sand his footsteps had disturbed scudding backwards down the side of the dune and feathering across his own hands as he sat there waiting. There was a pause, then the dune slid again and Roly was back at his side.

'It's OK, as good as empty. The sea's way out. There are a couple of people miles up the beach to the right but they don't count - they couldn't recognise us from that far even if they wanted to.'

'Miles? It doesn't go on for miles, does it?'

'That's what you think. Come on and see for yourself.'

Matthew grinned and held out his hand, and they scrambled on upward together until he felt the pull of the sand begin to lessen. Then the wind was there again to meet him, bringing new smells with it, grey-green smells, and he knew that the sea lay before him. The hand tightened on his sleeve, and they were at a standstill.

'There it is, Matt.'

Closing his eyes, he followed the words outward and seemed to see what Roly saw, though the voice at his side was silent. The emptiness of sand and sky meeting at last, far out, in the emptiness of water.

'How far is it, Roly?'

'Half a mile perhaps.'

'Can we reach it?'

'Of course we can, that's what we're here for. Come on.'

Matthew bounded behind him down the dune, stumbling helplessly in its deep dryness, then found himself without warning on level ground again. Together they set off into the wind with the sand growing firmer and wetter as they tore across it, until they were spraying up water at every step and Matthew came to a breathless halt.

'Are we there?'

'Where?'

'At the sea.'

'Nearly. A couple of hundred yards.'

'I can hear it. It's everywhere. Like the rushes.'

'I told you. Come on.'

'Just a sec.' He rolled up his jeans and fumbled at the laces of his trainers, then dragged off his socks, laughing aloud at the touch of naked sand on his feet. 'OK, ready!'

And he was there, almost before he knew it, splashing up salt across his face and catching his breath at the icy coldness of the water. He stepped out farther, thrilling as the shallow waves broke against his shins and hissed away up the beach, and waiting each time for them to recede again to the sea and suck his feet downward as they went. From behind him on the sand the sudden loudness of Roly's voice surprised him; he hadn't realised that the familiar hand was gone from his sleeve.

'Matt! Come here!'

'It's OK, I won't fall over.'

'Come *here!*'

The alarm in the voice startled him and he turned and made his way back across the few yards to the beach. Immediately, Roly's grasp was on his arm.

'What's up, Roly?'

'You were too far out!'

'What? It was only a few feet, it wasn't even up to my knees. Come on in, it's great.'

'No!'

'Why not? I thought that's why we'd come here?'

'I never said that!'

'I don't get it, Roly. What are we down here for then?'

'Because you wanted to come. I knew you wanted to come more than anything, so I brought you. But not to go in!'

He felt the hand tighten on his arm.

'But there's nothing to be scared of, is there? It won't hurt to go in a few feet. It's calm, isn't it?'

'You don't know it! You don't know it like I do!'

'But even if I fall over, it doesn't matter. I'm used to the water – Mum taught me. I can swim.' Then another thought struck him and he bit his lip, annoyed with himself for not having realised. He spoke gently. 'Can't you swim, Roly?'

'No.'

The voice was quiet now, but whether with shame or with fear Matthew couldn't tell. He paused, feeling suddenly wretched.

'Sorry, Roly. I should've asked. I won't go off again, I promise.'

Slowly the fingers relaxed their grip and he could sense that whatever feeling had possessed Roly a moment before had passed now, giving way to awkwardness and embarrassment.

Burrowing at the sand with his toes he waited for Roly to break the silence, wondering whether it would be with an explanation or just an apology. But it was neither. When Roly's voice came again, he looked up in surprise. It was as friendly and eager as if nothing had happened.

'How about heading up to the left a bit? We've easily got time for half a mile along the sea, then we can aim up the beach to the dunes and follow them back to where we started from.'

'Yes OK, Roly.'

'You don't sound very keen. You've only got to say if you'd rather do something else. It's your outing, Matt.'

'No, honestly, I'd love to.'

'Great. You'd better put your trainers back on then.'

'What?'

'You'd better put your trainers back on – there'll be bits of broken shells and things farther on.'

'Oh. Yes.'

He squatted down, unsure suddenly whether Roly had made the suggestion with the deliberate intention of keeping him from the sea. There was a gritty roughness of sand between his toes and across the top of his feet and he wondered if he should go back to the edge of the water and wash it off. But he decided against it. Pulling on his socks and shoes, he stood up again and smiled.

'OK, all set.'

And with Roly on the seaward side they set off to the west.

Eleven

Sunlight and shadows sped inward from the sea, he could sense them on his eyes as he ran across the sand to Roly. They brought salt with them too, and the smell of weed and water. He wondered suddenly if he'd ever felt happier.

'Roly!' He sat down, panting. 'Roly, what's this one? Is it another mussel? It feels like lots of them all joined together.'

'That's not a shell, Matt. It's a crab's claw.' Matthew threw it from him with a yell and rubbed his hand on his jeans. 'Hey, what did you do that for?'

'They pinch, don't they?'

'Not when they're dead, cretin.'

'How do you know it was dead, then?'

'Well it was hardly likely to be very alive, was it, if it was just a leg?'

Matthew rallied, grinning. 'It might've been. The rest of it might've just crawled inside its own leg to fool us.'

'You know, you're more of a genius than I reckoned.'

'Not really. Just a world expert on crabs, that's all.'

'OK, what else do you know about them, then?'

'Well they walk sideways for one thing.'

Roly snorted. 'No they don't.'

'They do! Mum told me.'

'Oh, mothers always come out with that sort of stuff. But they never bother to see it from the crab's point of view, do they?'

'What's that supposed to mean?'

'Well it's obvious, isn't it? From the crab's point of view it's us that walk sideways. I'd have thought any world expert would've known that. – Come on, let's head up towards the dunes again, there'll be lots more shells and things up there.'

With the wind gusting at his back Matthew followed him across the beach, scanning it with his feet as he went. Its surface surprised him. He remembered the level smoothness of his first run down to the sea, half a mile away to the east, and wondered why it was so different here, broken by such deep rifts and channels.

'What are all these sort of valleys, Roly? It wasn't like this before, was it?'

'They're inlets. There are more and more of them the farther you go up the coast. They come from right out under the sea.'

'Where do they end?'

'Up near the dunes. They sort of curve round and then run along in front of them. When the tide comes in, they're the first bit of the beach to fill up with water.'

'Do they fill up fast?'

'Yes, very.'

'But that's dangerous, isn't it? I mean, if you were down by the sea they could fill up behind you, couldn't they?'

'They could if you weren't watching out.'

Matthew shivered suddenly and turned his face back towards the water, listening.

'The tide's not coming in yet, is it?'

'No, stop worrying. I told you, I know it. And we're nearly across the last of them now anyway.'

In less than five minutes they had turned again towards the east, tracing their way back along the foot of the dunes. After a few yards Matthew had slackened his pace, frowning. Beneath the soles of his trainers the sand had grown sharp and brittle with new sounds.

'What are we walking on, Roly? It's like broken glass or something.'

'It's shells, I told you. Millions of them.'

'But why are they all here on this one bit of beach?'

'They're not. Look.' Matthew felt the familiar arm across

his shoulders, drawing him to a standstill and turning him in line with the coast. 'Look as far as you can, Matt, right along the sand at the bottom of the dunes. We could walk that far on shells all the way, and when we got there and looked again as far as we could, they'd still be going on ahead of us.'

And with Roly's eyes Matthew saw the shells before him like an endless ribbon, dividing the wet sand from the dry.

'Why, Roly?'

'It's the high-tide line. The sea brings them in with it and leaves them behind. Stranded like the boats were, remember?'

'But won't we break them if we walk on them?'

'Oh they're broken already, most of them. The waves smash them up till they're nothing but sand again.'

Matthew squatted down and stroked a wide arc with his fingers.

'Here's a whole one, I think. What sort is it?'

'Tell me.'

'It's a mussel, a big one.'

'That's right.'

'What about this one? I haven't had one like this before, have I?'

'No. It's a whelk-shell.'

'A whelk? We used to eat those in London, I think.' He smiled to himself at the sound of his own words. For an instant London and Byron Rise floated up among the shells, then fell away again into sand. 'Is there still a whelk inside it?'

'No such luck. It saw you coming probably.'

Matthew laughed, reading the shell over and over with his fingers.

'What colour is it, Roly?'

'I don't know. I think it's forgotten it ever had one. Don't worry though. When the sea touches it again, it'll remember.'

'Will the tide float it back out again, do you think?'

'It might. That's what it's waiting here for.'

Matthew paused and turned his head slowly. Something had caught his attention in Roly's last words. Not the words themselves but the way they'd been spoken. It had come again, the same note in the voice, quiet and strange as if a shadow had crossed it. He listened to its echo in his head, but its meaning remained hidden. So he answered softly, with senses alert.

'What if it doesn't, Roly? What if the tide doesn't reach it?'

The silence was endless. Roly's voice hardly broke it.

'I suppose it'll just go on hoping. That's all it can do.'

It was as if he had spoken the words to himself. The shadow would pass in a moment and the voice would brighten as if nothing had happened. But now it lay between them like something that couldn't be crossed or broken. Matthew waited for its passing, knowing there would be no more speaking until then, or sharing. The separation pained him.

The waiting grew longer. With a feeling almost of desperation he tried to recall the echo, to give a name to the shadow between them. He heard it again, as he'd heard it in the churchyard and the saltings, by the track leading down to the creeks. Not mistrust, or concealment. Something else, something deeper and darker. Like longing . . . And then, with a sudden startling sureness, he knew. It was sadness.

From somewhere far out, a wind brushed across his eyes. He closed them against it and the tears didn't come. But he felt them inside him.

He wondered if he'd ever heard such sadness before. But he couldn't remember. The time before Roly seemed like another world, too far away now to reach. He wondered if there was a reason for Roly's sadness, or if it was just part of him, like his happiness. Perhaps this world was just different from the one he'd left behind, that was all. Perhaps people here were different, with moods which changed more quickly. He remembered Mrs Weaver. And even things seemed different here, even things seemed to change. Like the Hall and the dyke. . . He was slightly cheered by the thought. It was so crazy. He waited again, stirring at the dust of shells.

With a sudden crunching underfoot, Roly stood up.

'We'll start heading back, Matt, shall we?'

It had passed. For the moment at least, the shadow had gone. If it came again, he'd try and understand it better. Until then, everything was all right. With a feeling almost of release, he scrambled to his feet.

'Great.'

'What's the latest your mum's expecting you?'

'Half past five, she said.'

'Oh we should do that all right. It's half a mile or so to where we came in, and then another three quarters of an hour to the churchyard. – Was she OK about it this time?'

'Fairly OK, after yesterday. She still worries though.'

'What's she doing this afternoon?'

'Sitting in the garden probably, with her feet up.'

'Doesn't she get bored doing nothing?'

Matthew laughed. 'No way. It's a real luxury for her, she says, not having to run around all day, and just doing things in her own time, without people yelling at her to get a move on. I wish she didn't have to go out to work, really. It'd have been different if I'd had a dad.'

'What happened to him?'

'He died just before I was born. It must've been terrible for Mum, what with that and then my eyes and everything.'

'Where does she work?'

'In London, in a canteen. She's a cook.'

The brief silence which followed surprised Matthew slightly; he had expected an answer, or another question perhaps. But his remark was left hanging in the air. He remembered suddenly what Mr Chapman had said about the Johnsons, that they owned a big house at the end of the village and that Mr Johnson was in business in Wells; and he wondered if Roly was shocked by how different their families were. Then he felt ashamed of the thought; Roly wasn't that sort of person.

He broke the silence himself. 'Mum's great, Roly, you'd really like her. I'd love you to meet her.'

Again Roly hesitated before answering. 'Yes, I bet she is.'

'I'd love it if. . .'

But before Matthew had time to repeat the second part of his remark, the subject was abruptly closed.

'Come on then, Matt, let's get moving, shall we?'

'Yes. . . Yes, OK.'

They set off once more along the beach, closing the circle of their visit. Roly talked eagerly as they went, describing the things he could see and the things he had seen and the things which others had seen before he was born. And all this Matthew saw too, hardly knowing at times whether what he saw was present or past. He saw the dunlin and sandpipers down by the water, and the pieces of amber cast up with the shells; the smugglers laden with brandy and tobacco, and their route across the dunes to Malham; and he saw the whale, too, as vast as a ship, washed ashore centuries ago by the tide.

Then they sat side by side in a hollow of the dune they had crossed an hour before and he closed his eyes, knowing that he was watching the same sea that Roly was watching though the voice was no longer speaking. He wondered if he would ever see it like this again.

'I hope I don't ever forget what it's like here, Roly. I don't think I will.'

'You won't forget. Nobody does once they've seen it.'

'I've forgotten London already.'

'It's different here. It leaves its marks on you.'

Matthew smiled and remembered the marks of the wind on the gravestones. Then he sat silent again and wondered whether that, too, could be looked at the other way round. Whether the gravestones left their marks on the wind.

'Perhaps it won't forget me then, either, when I'm gone. Perhaps I've sort of left my marks too. Do you think I have?'

'Look at the beach, Matt. Is it the same as before you came? You can see for yourself.'

And Matthew closed his eyes and saw how the emptiness of sand had changed. Two sets of footprints marked it now, from the dune to the sea, and didn't return.

'Are the other prints there as well, Roly? The ones we made along by the water?'

'Not now. The tide's come in a yard or two.'

'It must look so weird then. As if we'd gone on and on into the sea without stopping.'

There was a slight hesitation before Roly answered.

'Yes.'

'But they'll all be gone soon, won't they? When the tide goes out again it'll have washed them away.'

'No. It'll have buried them, that's all, like it buries everything. But they'll still be there.'

Matthew was startled. For the past half hour not a shadow had crossed their happiness. But now, without warning, it had returned. Again the voice had grown quiet and distant, as if Roly were lost in his own thoughts, unaware of the presence at his side. And Matthew knew now that he'd been right. There was sadness in the voice, deeper than anything he could understand. But he wanted to understand. He turned towards it slowly, as if afraid of frightening it into silence.

'Do you *like* the sea, Roly?'

'What makes you ask that?'

'I don't know. I wasn't sure, that's all.'

'I suppose I'm not sure either. Sometimes I don't, sometimes it scares me. But there are other times too, when I know it's the only thing I've ever really wanted.'

'How do you mean?'

'I can't explain. I'm scared of its touch, scared of what it can do. But I want to be part of it too.'

'I don't understand.'

'Look, Matt!' As if it was giving him an answer, the hand was suddenly on his shoulder guiding his eyes to the sea, the other arm outstretched. Puzzled, he turned his face back to the wind. Then his ears told him what it was he saw. A gull. The cry rose up from the water and echoed away into the sky. And for a moment he thought he understood what the cry had told him, though whether it was a cry of freedom or longing or sadness or joy, or all at once, he didn't know. But whatever it was he knew that he'd heard it before. He heard it again now, in the voice beside him. 'That's how I want to be, just like that! Just leaving the land behind like they do and not stopping, ever!' For an instant the voice fell away, then it rose once more on the wind. 'Do you know what people round here say about the gulls? Do you know what they say they are?'

'No. Tell me.'

'They say they're souls, Matt. Risen souls.'

Then the cry was silent again and Matthew was silent too, hardly knowing any more what he'd heard, only knowing it was time to go. He stood up.

'We'd better be off, Roly, hadn't we?'

Roly scrambled to his feet, dusting himself down. When he spoke, his voice held no shadow of the cry.

'You're right. We'll have to step on it now if we're going to be back on time.'

'I don't want to go really. It's been a great afternoon. I hate it when things end.' His words stirred a memory. 'Roly, did you know they're going to sell off the estate?'

'Yes.'

'And pull down the Hall?'

'Yes.'

'Don't you mind?'

'No, not really, I suppose.'

'I did, when I heard about it off Mrs Weaver. I don't know why. It just seems sort of sad somehow, after all these years. I can't explain really. It's as if everything's changing, or ending, or something. As if I won't ever be able to come back and see it all again.'

'*Have* you seen it, then? I mean, have you been there?'

'Where?'

'The Hall.'

'Well not exactly, I suppose. I've been past it with Mum a couple of times.'

'Would you like to? I'll show it to you if you want. We could go tomorrow if you're not doing anything. – You'd have to keep it quiet, mind.'

Matthew was taken aback. He had hardly dared hope for another afternoon with Roly; but the suggestion filled him with a vague sense of alarm.

'How do you mean?'

'Like I said. I'll show you round.'

'Inside?'

'Of course inside.'

'But it's locked, isn't it?'

'It's supposed to be. There's a broken window at the back though.'

'Have you been there before?'

Roly laughed. 'Oh yes, lots of times. How about it? You could tell your Mum we're going for a walk round the grounds – that wouldn't be lying, would it? And I'd really like to show it you.'

'But it's a ruin, isn't it? Is it safe?'

'Safe as houses.'

Matthew bit his lip. The friendly eagerness in the voice was hard to resist. And there was something else too: in spite of his alarm, he realised now that he really wanted to go there. It was as if he felt in some strange way that it would help him to understand things better. To understand Roly better.

He drew a deep breath and grinned. 'OK, Roly. I'm game.'

'Great! Hey, come on, we'd better get moving.'

And leaving the sea to bury their footprints, they clambered away up the dune.

Twelve

'What time is it, Mum?'

His mother's voice rose above the scratchings of the saucepan-cleaner.

'Two minutes after what it was when you last asked me. Half past one.'

'Are you sure?'

'Of course I'm sure. I'm looking at the clock, aren't I?'

'It might have stopped or something.' The scratchings quickened up. They sounded annoyed. 'Have I finished yet, Mum?'

'No you haven't. There's another cup in the back corner.' He fumbled his way across the draining-board with the wet tea-cloth. 'And mind you don't drop it, it's one of the cottage ones.'

'Is it? I thought you said you weren't going to use other people's things.'

'When?'

'Last Saturday, in the car. I thought you reckoned they'd all be covered in plague or something.'

'Don't be daft, Matt. I just thought they mightn't be clean, that's all.' The saucepan pumped up and down in the water a few times, then fell silent. 'It's funny, it seems different after a day or two, it all starts seeming like your own stuff. You know – as if you've always been using it.'

'Yes. I know.'

'I never thought I'd get used to it really, somebody else's house and everything. But it'll be almost funny going back now.'

'Oh don't let's talk about it, Mum. It's not yet.'

'It's not long though, is it? I've got to face that drive again the day after tomorrow. It seems to have flown by somehow.'

'Have I finished now?'

'Yes, I'll see to the saucepans. I don't want them done with the best tea-cloth.'

'Great. Where's my anorak?'

'Over on the chair where you left it. I'll have to see about affording you another one when we get home, it's that shabby. Goodness knows what people must think when they see it.'

'Oh don't worry, nobody's had the chance.' He bit his tongue and went on quickly. 'I mean, nobody'll have the chance today anyway. I told you, we're just going for a walk round the grounds.'

'What time are you going to be back?'

'About five if that's OK.'

'I'm popping down for a cup of tea with Mrs Edwards a bit later on, but I'll be back by then. They're a nice lot of people round here, I'll say that for them. I'll miss them when we go.'

'Yes. So will I.'

'Who'd have thought it a week ago? Like a real lady of leisure I am. It'll spoil me for that canteen all right. Bring me my bag off the table, Matt, and I'll give your hair a bit of a comb.'

'Oh, Mum, I'm not going to a funeral or anything.'

'That's as may be. – Hold still for goodness' sake, or it'll hurt even more.'

'I'll be bald in a minute.'

'It's tangled up from all that salt yesterday. Still, it's put that much colour in your cheeks nobody'll recognise you by the time we get home. – There.'

'Can I go now?'

'I suppose so. Now you're sure you're staying inside the grounds?'

'Yes, I told you.'

'Well, that's a weight off my mind anyway. I was that

worried yesterday.'

'I don't see why. I bet Roly knows more about the sea than anybody else does round here. He's down there nearly every day.'

'Maybe he is, but it didn't stop me worrying. Still, never mind, I can relax a bit today and enjoy my tea, knowing you're only nearby.'

Matthew paused suddenly at the door, as if her words held him back. He fingered the latch for a moment without speaking.

'What is it, love? I thought you were wanting to get started?'

'Yes, I am.' He turned back towards her awkwardly. 'Mum, thanks for letting me go off and everything. I didn't really mean what I said a minute ago, about you being daft to worry. I'd have hated it if I'd been the one left here and you'd kept on going off without me. It can't have been much fun for you this week.'

'Oh Matt, it has, it's been a lovely week! It's just that, well, . . .'

He knew what she was trying to say. It was what he'd tried to say himself, yesterday on the beach.

'I know, Mum. You'd like to have met him.'

'Well, yes, I suppose that's it really. It's not that I haven't trusted him, Matt, don't get that idea, mind. From what you've said, I don't think you could've found anybody nicer. But perhaps I'd just've liked to feel you'd want to bring him here, that's all. To meet me.'

'I do want to. I told him yesterday.'

The pleasure in her voice was unmistakable. 'Did you? What did he say?'

Matthew remembered the moment. He was puzzled again by Roly's reaction and, for the first time, slightly hurt by it. He wondered if it was the same kind of hurt his mother had been feeling.

'He said he bet you were great.'

'Did he? Blimey, I've got a lot to live up to all right. When's he coming?'

The question took him by surprise. 'Oh, I'm going to fix it today when I see him. I thought I'd better ask you first.'

'Goodness, you needn't have done that. I'd have put off anything else I might've been doing. Let's see now – I know! Let's have him to tea with us tomorrow, shall we? It'd be a real treat for our last day, wouldn't it? We'll go shopping in the morning, and I'll make something special. How would that be?'

'It'd be great, Mum, it really would.'

'That's so long as he's not doing anything else of course. I wouldn't want him to feel he *had* to come.'

Matthew felt suddenly determined that he'd make it work, for her sake as well as for his own.

'He'll want to come all right, you'll see.' He grinned and left the kitchen, then put his head back round the door.

'And Mum. . .'

'What is it?'

'Thanks again.'

And before she could answer, he'd gone.

'OK - down!' They tumbled together against the wall and flattened their backs to it, listening. Beyond, the familiar sounds of voices and traffic went on undisturbed. Roly spoke in a low whisper. 'Right, you'd better tuck your jeans inside your socks and keep as much of your hands inside your sleeves as you can. There'll be nettles most of the way.'

'Which way are we going, then?'

'Round the edge of the estate, inside the wall. Along this side by the street, then up the lane till we hit the path you used with your mum on Sunday, through the trees. We can't risk crossing open ground or we're bound to get spotted.'

'But there won't be anybody around, will there?'

‘There won’t be once we get up near the Hall.’

‘That only leaves the cottages then, doesn’t it? And Mrs Weaver hardly ever goes out.’

‘There’s your mum though, isn’t there? We don’t want her to see us, do we?’

Matthew wondered suddenly why they didn’t want her to see them, it didn’t seem to make much difference one way or the other. But he decided not to press the point.

‘No, OK.’

‘We’ll have to keep crouched down for the first bit, up as far as the main driveway. Once we’ve crossed it the wall gets higher and we’ll be able to walk upright – on tiptoe probably, because the nettles get higher there too. I’ll have to go in front for a change, so hang on to the back of me with your left hand and keep your right arm close to the wall. – I’ll do my best to clobber the nettles, but whatever you do don’t yell out if they get you. OK?’

‘OK.’

‘Come on then – and good luck. You’ll need it.’

‘Thanks. Same to you.’

Clinging to the hem of Roly’s jacket Matthew followed as best he could, bent double to make sure he was out of sight from the road. At first there was nothing but laughter inside him. He tried to imagine that there wasn’t a wall there at all and pictured the faces of the people on the opposite pavement as they watched him go by. Then the way grew denser and his laughter faded. A new feeling took its place, half excitement, half fear. Their hiding wasn’t a game any more, it was real. They were trying to reach a forbidden place.

Roly stopped suddenly and pulled him into leaves. He flinched away, shielding his face from their sting.

‘Sorry, Matt, I should’ve said – it’s OK, they’re not nettles, just some sort of bush or other. We’ve reached the drive. Hang on a sec and I’ll make sure it’s clear.’

The branches swished aside and fell back like a curtain, leaving him alone. For an instant he held his breath, straining his ears to catch something of Roly's whereabouts. But the bush remained silent. Then, without warning, it exploded against him. The noise of it struck him like a blow, drowning his own scream as it hurtled past him. Immediately, the bush moved again. He threw himself backwards in terror, then clung to the arm round his shoulders.

'It's OK, Matt. It's OK, it's gone now. Listen.'

And Matthew heard it swooping away through the leaves, whirring like clockwork.

'What was it, Roly, for God's sake?'

'Come on, you can stop trembling now. It was only a pigeon.'

'A *pigeon*? You've got to be joking!'

'It was a wood-pigeon, that's all.'

'What *size* was it?'

'Well, pigeon-size. About twenty times smaller than you, I should think.'

'Blimey, it sounded big enough to be a pterodactyl or something. I've never heard anything like it.'

'Oh they always make that sort of cretinous din when they're scared.'

Matthew laughed suddenly. 'They're not the only ones, are they? I should think the whole village heard me.'

'Come on then, let's get going before they turn up. The driveway was clear a minute ago.'

In less than quarter of an hour they had turned the north-west corner and were heading up rising ground towards the path through the trees. Roly had been right, the nettles were shoulder-high here. He moved forward slowly, trampling great swathes of them away from the wall. They were everywhere. Matthew could smell the sharp green smells of their breaking. The leaves touched his hands gently but the pain came when the touch had gone, hot and cold in his whole body. He shrank against Roly and waited for the sound of the trees.

It came at last as it had on Sunday, filling the sky with rushes. They walked beneath it, side by side now on the broad shadows of the gravel, and Matthew felt a new tingle in his body which wasn't the tingle of nettles.

'Are we nearly there, Roly? Can you see the garden?'

'Soon now.'

As the hand on his sleeve led him nearer, the memory of Sunday sharpened. He clenched his eyes and saw again what he thought he'd seen then, the Hall and the garden and the pillared doorway. He wondered if the same thing would happen today and what Roly would say if he told him. Then before he knew it the footsteps beside him had halted and he halted with them and opened his eyes. The greyness of shadows gave way to the greyness of sunlight and he smiled, knowing that this time there'd be no deception.

'Here we are, Matt. It's the garden. We've made it.'

'Yes.' He spoke as quietly as Roly, and drew closer to his shoulder. 'Tell me what it's like.'

'It's a wilderness. Just grass and bushes.'

'Aren't there any flowers left now?'

'No, not any more.'

Matthew heard the sadness of the place in the voice at his side.

'It hasn't always been like this though, Roly, it was beautiful once. Mrs Weaver told me.'

'Yes.'

'That's why it seems such a pity somehow, seeing it so dead and forgotten and everything, and knowing it's all going to go. It's funny to think of the people who've been here, isn't it? I bet it remembers all of them. Perhaps it's a bit like our footprints on the beach when the tide's gone out again. Perhaps they're all still here even if we can't see them.' His own idea made him shiver slightly and he grinned it away. 'I hope they're not though. You don't think there'll be anybody at home, do you?'

'No. Not yet anyway.'

'How do you mean?'

'Well, we'll be there in a minute ourselves. We'll be the last ones to set foot there, probably.' His voice brightened suddenly. 'Let's go and give it a bit of life again, shall we, before it goes?'

Matthew hesitated, aware again of the vague unease he had felt yesterday on the beach when the suggestion had first been made.

'Do you really think we ought to, Roly?'

'Well of course I do! That's why we've come here, isn't it? It'll love it. It'll be just like the old days for it, all over again. Come on, let's go and open up. It's all ours now, for the last time.'

Thirteen

The Hall was dead, he was sure it was. He had felt it from the moment he came in. He felt it again now, as he stood in silence in the vast hallway which had once been the heart of the house. Its heart seemed to have stopped. He remembered the eager brightness of Roly's words ten minutes ago in the garden. *Let's go and give it a bit of life again, shall we?* But perhaps it was already too late.

His whisper echoed in emptiness.

'It's really weird, Roly, like being in a tomb or something. It's so dead.'

'No it's not. It's sleeping, that's all.'

Matthew smiled uneasily. 'Won't we wake it?'

'Of course not. We're just part of its dream.'

He listened again to the silence and felt himself shiver. 'You don't come here on your own, do you?'

'Yes, often.'

'I wouldn't, not if I was paid to. It's so lonely.'

'Yes. I thought it'd be different today though, with you here.'

'And is it?'

'I'm not sure yet. – Hey, you're not sorry you came, are you?'

'No, of course I'm not. I've been wondering what it was like ever since last Saturday. But I never thought it'd be like this.'

'What did you think it'd be like?'

'I don't know really.' He frowned, remembering how his eyes had tricked him on Saturday and Sunday, and saw it again for a moment as he'd seen it then, bright against the darkness and bright with sunlight. 'Perhaps I thought it'd be more like it must have been in the old days.' Then he frowned again, puzzled by the connection of his own ideas.

'You can still sense how grand it was though, can't you, even now. This hallway takes up the whole of the middle of the house – it goes all the way up to the roof.' The familiar hand was on his shoulder, guiding his eyes. 'Look – right up to the top as far as you can, where the ceiling curves into a dome – you can see the big iron ring where the chandelier used to hang.'

'How do you get to the other floors?'

'Bring your eyes down from the dome to the two galleries running right round the walls, one below the other. There's one for each floor – the corridors lead off from them. And here's the main staircase facing us, up to the first gallery. I bet it's the widest staircase in the world – you could drive a carriage up it if you wanted to.'

'Mrs Weaver told me about the carriages and everything, coming up the drive for parties and things. It must've been great.'

'Yes.'

'Do you think they had the dances here, where we're standing now?'

'Of course. It's the biggest bit of the whole house, I told you.'

Matthew turned in a slow circle, reading the vastness of the place in the echo of his footsteps. 'It's so hard to imagine it now, isn't it?'

The hand was on his sleeve again. 'It is from down here. Come on, let's go up to the first gallery.'

'What?'

'I said let's go upstairs. It'll be better from up there.'

'Is it safe, Roly?'

'Of course it's safe. It was built to last longer than this, wasn't it?' With a strange feeling of anxiety and excitement, Matthew let himself be guided to the foot of the staircase. 'OK, now it's twenty steps up, then right, then another fifteen to the gallery. All set?'

'Yes.'

And he began to climb, sliding his trainers slowly forward across each tread. Beneath his soles, dust grated on wood. If he turned, his footprints would be there behind him as they had been yesterday on the beach. And they would still be there even when the dust had buried them again. He wondered whose footprints lay buried beneath his own.

'Here we are, Matt, it's the gallery. Hang onto the rail and look down.'

He clung to the grittiness of wood, glad of its support against his chest. Beyond it, he could hear the hallway plunging downward into space.

'We're so high up, Roly!'

'Yes, we're above the chandelier now, so we can't be seen.'

'But there isn't a chandelier here now, is there?'

'There is if we want there to be. There's nothing to stop us seeing *anything* if we want to, is there?'

Matthew grinned. He felt suddenly as breathlessly happy as if Roly had given him eyes. He wondered if he'd ever feel so happy with anyone again. 'No,' he said. 'No, there isn't.'

'Crouch down then, and look at the hallway through the bars of the balustrade. It's better from up here, like I said, – you can see it all at one go.'

Matthew crouched down and pressed his face between the bars. He closed his eyes and smiled. Far below the darkness of the gallery he could see the hallway, bright in the light of the chandelier.

'Listen, Matt! Can you hear the sounds on the gravel? They're coming!'

Matthew felt his heartbeat quicken, and his hands tightened on the bars. He could hear them, set spinning by the words in his ear, the sounds of wheels on gravel.

'It's the carriages, Roly, isn't it? The carriages are coming!'

'And so many of them! It's a party, Matt - there's going to

be a party! Here's the butler now and the footman, they've heard it too. Can you see them hurrying across to the door?'

'They're opening it now, aren't they? And the guests are coming in!'

'Yes. Look!'

And Matthew listened to Roly's voice and saw them, as Mrs Weaver had listened to her grandmother's voice long ago and seen them too. He saw ladies in silk dresses in the brightness below him, and gentlemen in tailcoats, and champagne flowing like water. And he saw the Latimers too, grand and wealthy, sweeping through the hallway to receive their guests.

'Where are the children, Roly? Are they down there too?'

'They're here beside us, Matt! It's too dark to see them but they're here. They've crept out of bed and they're here, waiting for the music. Watching in secret, like we are. Listen! It's starting!'

But Matthew had heard it already, the music they were all waiting for, swirling with the dresses in the hallway and up towards him until his head was swirling with it and he sat back on his heels in the grit and laughed. At his side, Roly was laughing too. And their laughter awoke old echoes before it died away into the dome.

'I bet it was just like that, Roly, I bet it really was! It must've been fantastic to have been up here seeing it all, mustn't it?'

'Yes. It must have.'

Then the silence began to settle again and Roly stood up. 'Come on, let's go and have a look at the rooms on this floor. There's not much left to see but we might as well while we're here.'

They made their way along the corridor which led off the gallery. Roly pushed open door after door and they went through each one and lingered for a moment, deciding what the room had been. They found the drawing-room and the dining-room, and a library of empty shelves. Then there were others whose use had been long forgotten, where the damp was hanging like fog. All were different in size but the same in their smell of decay, and all were loud with the same broken sounds underfoot, like the shells on the beach.

They reached the gallery again and paused.

'What now, Roly? Have we finished?'

'No, not yet. There's another floor, I told you.'

'But isn't it just the same as this one?'

'Sort of. But it's got my favourite room in. Come on, I can't leave without saying hello to it.'

For the first time since they'd left the hallway, Matthew felt a stir of unease.

'Is there anything inside it?'

'No, why? It's as empty as all the others.'

'What's so special about it then?'

'I don't know really. I just like it, that's all. I want to show it you.'

In spite of Roly's eagerness Matthew was surprised to feel his unease increasing as they moved on round the gallery to its farther side. He frowned, wondering why. Following slowly, he listened to the echoes their footsteps roused in the empty boards. Then their note changed.

'Here's the final staircase, Matt, up to the corridor. Soon be there now.'

One step at a time, his feet fumbled their way upward. With every step the feeling of apprehension tightened on his chest. It was as if, in some strange way, this wasn't a game any more. As if. . . They had arrived at the top. Suddenly he wrenched free of Roly's hand and drew back, breathless.

'Hey, what's up, Matt?'

For a long moment he didn't answer. He remained where he was, staring ahead into greyness. Then, with an effort, he managed to speak.

'I'm not sure. Sorry, Roly, it's just all this dust probably. My eyes felt a bit giddy or something.'

He heard Roly hesitate. When his voice came again there was real concern in it, and an attempt to conceal disappointment.

'Would you rather get back outside, Matt? It doesn't matter, honestly. We don't have to go on if you don't want to, it's not that important.'

Matthew bit his lip. 'No it's OK, it's gone now.' It had gone. Whatever it was, it had passed. It was all right again now. He forced himself to smile. 'Another few minutes won't hurt, will they? Anyway, I want to see this room of yours.'

'Great. Come on then, I'll lead the way. We're just at the opening of the corridor – the room's right at the far end, facing us.'

'What's the corridor like?'

'What?'

'The corridor. What's it look like?'

'Same as all the others, damp and dark. Why?'

'Oh nothing. I just wondered, that's all.'

But he didn't tell Roly why he wondered. He didn't tell him that he thought he'd already seen it, back there at the top of the stairs. A fraction of a second perhaps, like the Hall and the dyke, no longer than it took to dream. But it had been enough for the image to take shape in his mind. He clenched his eyes to recall it, to see if he'd been right, and it returned for an instant, real and unreal, like a dream on waking. The dream of a corridor bright with candles and his own feet running towards the farthest doorway, desperate to reach the room beyond. Then the candlelight flickered and the image faded into greyness. He followed Roly in silence.

'Here we are then.'

The corridor had ended. His heartbeat quickened again and he stopped and waited for the door to open. It grated on fallen plaster and he stepped forward, knowing that he'd reached the room. But though the shadows lightened on his eyes, it remained as closed to him as all the others had.

His breathing relaxed. The strangeness of the moment had passed for good.

Roly wandered across to the window, crunching echoes underfoot. Then he turned round again and chuckled.

'Well here it is, as empty as all the others, just like I said, and no funny surprises.'

'No.'

'Relieved?'

'I don't know really. – Yes, I think I am a bit.' He laughed suddenly, feeling glad to have made the confession.

'There, that's more like it. You're feeling OK now, aren't you?'

'Yes. Yes I am. I'm sorry about back there, Roly, it was daft. I can't explain. It's my eyes, I think. They do weird things sometimes. Anyway, forget it, it's over now – so you can tell me what's so great about this room now you've dragged me all the way up here. What sort of room was it, d'you reckon?'

'A bedroom. We're on the top floor, remember? Come on into the window and I'll show you one reason I like it.'

The window-seat was deep, and crusty with grit. They knelt on it, facing out. But Roly didn't need to show him what it was that he saw. He knew. He could see it in the light on his eyes, grey-green, though whether it was the light of sea or sky there was no way of telling. But it didn't matter; from here they were both one. It was the same view they had had yesterday, sitting together in the hollow of the dune, when the bird had risen up from the water. And he knew now why Roly liked it. The window had left the land behind. It was as high as the gulls.

'There, Matt, now you know.'

'Yes.'

They knelt in silence. Matthew leaned his forehead against the window, smelling the oldness that his breath awakened in the glass. Then he lifted his finger and traced out a face in the mist. He sat back on his heels.

'Can you see it, Roly?'

'Yes. Who is it?'

'Me. To show I've been here.'

'It's gone now. Your breath's melted.'

'It hasn't really. Mum told me – if I breathe on it again, it'll still be there.' He smiled. 'Like the footprints in the sand, remember?'

They spoke for a while of other things, of the sea and the creeks and Malham. Their thoughts drifted back to the Hall again and Matthew told Roly what he'd learnt of the Latimers from Mrs Weaver. But though Roly listened with interest, he added nothing new to the tale. Then they had finished speaking but went on kneeling, knowing that if they stood up it would be time to leave.

It was Roly who broke their silence. 'What are you thinking, Matt?'

'Oh, I'm not sure really. About this week and the sea and the Latimers and everything, I suppose.' He paused again, feeling the quiet sadness of the place. Roly had been right. It wasn't dead, but sleeping. Dreaming old memories. 'I think I was wondering if people had knelt here in the old days, like we are, seeing the same things we're seeing now. Do you think they did?'

'They're bound to have. It's the same window and the same sea. Nothing's changed.'

'It's funny to think of, isn't it? I wonder who they were. Do you think this was a children's room, Roly? I don't know why really, but it feels as if it was somehow. Do you think it was children kneeling here?'

'Yes.'

The same faint note had returned to the voice, with its strange sadness. But this time Matthew wasn't startled by it. It was easier to understand now, somehow. It was part of the sadness he felt himself, the strange sadness of the Hall.

'How can you be so sure, Roly?'

'Breathe on the glass again, then you'll know.'

Matthew smiled and thought he understood. He leaned forward. His breath filled the glass. And though his eyes were closed he saw his own face again in the mist, and there were other faces with it, the faces of other children, showing him they'd been here. Then the window freed them and they were sky again.

He sat back slowly, remembering something.

'Do you know what I think, Roly?'

'No.'

'I think this was Rupert's room.'

'What?'

'Rupert. I'd forgotten all about it. It was the gravestone I was reading in the churchyard that first day. Have you seen it?'

'Yes.'

'If this was the children's room, it was his too. I'd like to think it was, somehow. D'you reckon it could have been?'

'Perhaps.' Roly stood up. The movement was so abrupt that Matthew felt the jolt of it in his whole body. The stillness was broken. 'Come on, Matt, it's time we were getting back.' His footsteps crunched swiftly away towards the door and halted there, waiting. 'Are you coming?'

For a moment Matthew remained where he was, unsure what had happened. Then he hoisted himself unsteadily down from the window-seat and followed. Roly's hand met him and tightened on his sleeve.

'What's up, Roly?'

'How do you mean?'

'It was just a bit sudden, that's all. I didn't expect you to jump up so soon.'

'Well we don't want to be late, do we? Or your mum'll worry.'

'I suppose so, yes.' He paused again, then turned back slowly to the room as if trying to imprint it on his memory.

'It's great here, Roly. Thanks for showing it me. It's sad in a way, having to leave and everything, when I was just beginning to get to know it.'

'Yes.'

The hand on his sleeve turned him quickly away and steered him out into the blind shadows of the corridor. Before he had time to look back, the door was dragged shut.

He saved the invitation until the last moment, by the churchyard wall. He wasn't sure why. Perhaps because he had the odd feeling that Roly might refuse.

It was Roly himself who gave him the opening he wanted, as they were saying goodbye.

'We haven't decided about tomorrow yet, Matt. You're sure you want to meet up again?'

'You bet I am. It'll be the last chance, won't it?'

'I know.'

'Have you got anything planned, Roly?'

'No, not specially. It ought to be your choice tomorrow, oughtn't it, seeing it's the only day left. Is there anything you'd really like to do?'

'Yes. Yes, there is.'

'Great. Just say the word then.'

Matthew hesitated. 'Roly, if there's something I'd like to do more than anything else, would you promise to say yes?'

'Of course I would. I've told you, I'll go anywhere you want. Come on, Matt, just say it.'

'OK then. I want you to come to tea. To meet Mum.'

When the silence came, he knew that he'd somehow expected it. But he hadn't known that he'd find it so painful. Somewhere nearby, a bee fidgeted its way across lavender, then faded beyond the church.

'Roly, are you still there? – Roly?'

'Yes.'

'Roly, you promised.'

'I know.'

'You do want to meet Mum, don't you?'

'Yes.'

'Four o' clock then? Up at the cottage, OK?'

'Yes.'

In spite of the quietness of the words, Matthew felt suddenly relieved. It was going to be all right.

'It'll be great, don't worry. Mum's really nice, you'll see. And you can hear my cassettes and things if you like. Or I could teach you to read a bit of Braille with your fingers, I bet you'd soon pick it up. – Roly?'

But Roly had already gone.

Fourteen

'Here's the spray, Matt. You can give this table a bit of a polish for me before I put the cloth on.'

'Blimey, Mum, he's not going to look under the tablecloth, is he?'

'That's all very well, but I like to have things nice. And mind you feel which way the nozzle goes or you'll have polish all over your T-shirt.'

'OK, I'm not daft, am I?'

She bustled away into the kitchen again and her bustle told him how excited she was. He grinned to himself and squirted the polish. Then he swore under his breath and rubbed at his chest with the duster.

Her voice came hollow, talking in private with the kitchen cupboard: 'D'you reckon we ought to use the cottage cups? They're a bit better than ours.'

'I should use ours if I was you. We don't want to send him home with plague.' Then he chuckled to himself. Cups were coming out of the cupboard with a cautious tinkle. The cottage ones.

She reappeared in the sitting-room with the cups still tinkling.

'There, love, that's grand. You can see your face in it.'

The tablecloth blew washing-powder across the room, and there was a rattle of tea-plates. Then cellophane.

'What's that, Mum?'

'What's what?'

'The packet you're opening.'

'Serviettes, from the village this morning.'

'Blimey, I thought it was just Roly coming. You should've told me you'd asked the Queen as well and I'd have changed my jeans.'

The cellophane ignored him. 'Goodness, I didn't think they'd be this small the price I paid for them. They're not big enough to blow your nose in.'

'Oh I shouldn't worry, he probably won't want to. He'll probably bring his hankie with him.'

'Very funny, you're that sharp I'm surprised you weren't born in a knife-box. And that reminds me, we'd better have the best ones. Get them out for me, will you?'

'The best what?'

'Knives, I just said. They're in the box behind the armchair, we haven't unpacked them yet.'

'I didn't know we'd got any best ones.'

'Well of course we have. They're the ones we always have when we have people, the ones with bone handles.'

'They sound a bit gruesome to me. Anyway, why can't we just have the normal ones?'

'Use a bit of sense, Matt, we can't give people those, can we? I got them with petrol.'

'Well I've always had to have them. I don't get given these skeleton ones.'

'You're different.'

She was back in the kitchen before he could think of an answer. He began to unwrap the paper parcels of knives, thinking of Christmas. It *was* a bit like Christmas in a way, even the smells were the same.

'Hey, what's the smell, Mum? Is it a cake?'

'It might be.'

'Is it the sort with orange and chocolate in?'

'It might be.'

'Great!'

'I hope it's done all right, the knobs on this cooker are that daft. I hope it's not gooey or anything.'

'I like it gooey.'

He was glad she was as nervous as he was himself, it

made things easier somehow. But he was glad too that she didn't know why he was nervous. He remembered Roly's hesitation about meeting her, on the beach on Wednesday, and yesterday in the churchyard, and the memory tugged at his stomach.

'Blimey, it *is* a bit gooey, Matt. And that chocolate was ever so dear.'

He wondered if Roly had felt that he'd be out of place here, with his mother, in a cottage instead of a big house at the end of the village. Then he thrust the thought aside quickly and clattered the knives across the table. Roly was shy, that was all, but he'd soon get over it. Nobody was shy with his mother for long, because she never noticed.

Another tray arrived and unloaded itself.

'What's this lot, Mum?'

'Bread and butter and things, and the little cakes.'

'The iced ones?'

'That's right. You'll be able to tell Roly you iced them yourself.'

'I should think he'll be able to see that without being told. Are they really freaky?'

'Of course they're not, they're lovely. Now I think that's nearly everything apart from the dish for the jam.'

'What's the dish for?'

'For the jam, I told you.'

'We don't usually have a dish, do we?'

'Oh, Matt, don't show me up. Of course we have a dish when there're people.'

'There aren't people though, are there? There's only Roly.'

'Well that's the same, isn't it? I expect he's used to nice things. He's from a nice family, from what Mr Chapman said.'

'Yes.'

'Has he talked about them a lot?'

'No, not at all really.'

'Haven't you asked?'

'No, I suppose I haven't. I didn't really like to.'

'Why on earth not?'

'Oh I don't know. Perhaps he doesn't hit it off with them very well or something, or he'd have told me about them, wouldn't he? I've told him loads about you.'

'What've you been telling him?'

'Oh, about home and where you work and everything. That sort of stuff.'

'I hope you told him it's quite a nice canteen.'

'Yes of course I did. And it wouldn't bother him even if it wasn't, he's not snobby or anything.' He went on quickly, to avoid the memory of Roly's hesitation. 'What's the time, Mum?'

'Goodness, it's nearly ten to four and here's me still in my old scruff. You put the kettle on for me, while I go and doll myself up a bit.'

'There's no need to, Mum, honestly. I bet he won't notice one way or the other.'

'But I will, won't I? I can't sit down to tea looking like this, can I?'

'You usually do.'

'Oh Matt, stop being daft. You know it's supposed to be special. Anybody'd think you didn't *want* me to enjoy myself a bit.'

He listened for a moment to her quick footsteps on the stairs and across the upper landing. Coat-hangers jangled in the wardrobe. She was putting on her other dress, the special one, the one she wore when she went out. With a feeling of sudden unease, he hurried out into the kitchen and filled the kettle, glad of the din the water made as it began to boil. It drowned the echo of her last words. She was wrong. More than anything else in the world he did want her to enjoy herself. He wondered if that was why he felt so uneasy. The water rose in pitch and clicked off into silence. Behind him, the kitchen clock began to tick again. Her footsteps returned.

'There, now I'm ready.' She came across to him and smoothed his hair. Her touch left a scent of hand-cream. 'You're not looking much in the party spirit.'

'Oh I am. I was just thinking, that's all.'

'What about?'

'Just about the tea and everything, and Roly coming here. It seems funny somehow. I can't sort of imagine him with people around – you know, making polite conversation and that sort of stuff.'

'I expect he'll manage all right.'

'Yes, I suppose so. – Mum, you won't expect too much, will you? I mean, you won't be disappointed if he's quiet or anything, will you? I think he's a bit shy really.'

'Of course I won't be disappointed. There won't be much time for talking anyway, once we get stuck into this.' The larder door snapped shut, sending another gust of Christmas out across the kitchen.

'What is it, Mum? It's not *trifle*, is it?'

'It could be, couldn't it.' He heard the pleasure in her voice. 'I just hope I haven't put too much sherry in, that's all, we don't want to send him home squiffy. Still, I thought it'd be a bit of a special treat.'

Matthew reached out suddenly and put his arm round her, grinning.

'Thanks, Mum. It's all perfect, it really is.'

Behind his grin, tears were coming, but he didn't know why. Perhaps because it was all *too* perfect.

'Go on with you, you daft thing. And if you don't mind out, we'll be eating it off the floor. You go and put it on the table for me while I make the tea, and give me a shout when you hear him coming.'

He waited by the open window, perched on the sill. Somewhere out there, on grass or on gravel, the footsteps would be already approaching. Behind him in the kitchen the lid rattled into place on the teapot. Everything was ready. It was time.

He turned back to the room for a moment, wondering how it would sound a few minutes from now when Roly was in it. He listened, trying to imagine the voice, to hear if it was cheerful or quiet. But the room seemed to give him no answer, the voice remained silent. His feeling of unease returned as if he somehow knew that the room *had* answered after all, that the silence was its answer. He turned away from it and leaned across the sill.

The wind had moved far out, into the sea and rushes, leaving the land empty. Its emptiness frightened him suddenly, like the silence behind him. It seemed as empty as if no one had ever set foot there, or ever could. He sat back quickly and closed the window, to shut out what the stillness was telling him. But it was too late. It had told him already. He knew now for sure what was going to happen. The certainty numbed him.

'What is it, Matt? Is he coming?'

'No. No, he's not.'

No, he wasn't. Roly wasn't coming. He wasn't coming at all.

They waited together, their faces turned away from each other, not speaking. The silence was terrible, but words would have been worse. Words would have made Roly's absence real, they'd have been the end of waiting.

She was behind him now, on the sofa. The pages of her magazine flapped over and over, too fast for reading. Then they were still. With a cautious rustle her dress tautened and twisted, round towards the window. He could feel her eyes on him. He was glad he couldn't see them. The dress sighed again and turned back. Her fingers fidgeted with its creases, to smooth them. Her best dress, for tea with Roly. In the kitchen the clock ticked loudly, telling them both what they wouldn't tell each other.

Matthew stood up. His voice sounded too loud and jolly, like Mr Chapman's.

'He's late, Mum.'

'He is a bit. Perhaps he's been held up or something.' He could hear her trying to smile. 'Never mind, though, I can always make another pot of tea, can't I?' The smile trembled slightly and she paused, to steady it before going on. 'You *did* tell him four, didn't you? I know what an old empty-head you are.'

'Yes.' He hesitated, afraid of his next question. 'What's the time, Mum?'

'Let's see now. . . Oh, it's only about half past.'

His breath tightened. Half past four. He hadn't realised it could be so late. He turned away from her towards the table. The smell of trifle and cakes blew against his face, sweet and sickly.

'We could always start, love, just the two of us. There'll be plenty left over – for when he comes, I mean. I've made that much. It was a bit daft really, what with us going home tomorrow and everything. But you know what I'm like once I get going on something a bit special.' She laughed, and he heard the hurt behind it.

He clung to the edge of the table, trying to say yes, knowing how happy she'd be if he ate. She wouldn't care any more, about the time she'd spent, or the money. Perhaps he could pretend, as he had at Southend when she'd bought him the ice-creams she couldn't afford. He could pretend, and she'd be happy. . . The smell gusted up at him again and he clenched his teeth against it and knew there could be no pretending. His throat was full of tears.

'I couldn't, Mum, not yet, honestly.'

She gave no answer and he felt her helplessness. With one last effort of his whole body he turned again to face her, and grinned.

'We can't start without him, Mum, it'd spoil it. I bet he's on his way, I bet he'll kill himself when he sees what he's been missing. He's probably scared to come now or something, what with the time and everything – he's dead shy, I told you. Look, you wait here and I'll fetch him, OK?'

'Fetch him from where, Matt?' Her voice was dazed and anxious.

He moved towards the door, knowing only that he had to escape, to be on his own.

'I bet he'll come up through the churchyard, Mum. I bet he's coming now. I won't be a minute, OK? It'll be great, honestly.'

And before she knew what to say, he'd left her.

Racing the final few steps, he threw himself down by the wall of the churchyard. He pressed his face hard against its roughness, glad of the pain in his cheek and forehead. It took away the pain from inside him.

For a minute he stayed there, huddled against the stone. Then his face was numb, and the hurting inside him returned. Worse now, not better. In the cottage the pain he'd felt had been only for his mother. Here it was for Roly too, for the friendship that he knew was over.

He bit his lip, fighting back the tears that were going to come. Perhaps it wasn't true, perhaps his mother had been right even if she hadn't meant it, perhaps he'd been held up, was on his way. . . He *had* to be. With a sudden desperate hope he spun round and scrambled to his feet. Then his heart missed a beat. Somewhere in the greyness beyond the wall, something had moved. The shadow of a footstep, no more. But enough.

'Roly?'

He strained his ears, waiting. The silence was loud with his own pulsebeat. Nothing else. But there *had* been something. There was something again now. . . Not a movement, but something in the silence itself. A watchfulness.

'Roly?'

His cry echoed away into emptiness. Somewhere beyond the church a bird shifted in leaves. A car approached the stillness, swooped across it, left it behind. No sound now. Only the silence again, like a living presence, holding its breath...

A new feeling took hold of him, but whether of fear or joy or anger he didn't know. All he knew, with a certainty which overwhelmed him, was that someone was there. It had to be Roly. Wildly he dragged himself up onto the wall and dropped into the churchyard beyond.

For a few seconds he crouched there, until his panting subsided. He listened.

'Roly? Are you there?'

His whisper was answered by another, not a voice but a whisper of grass, as if the silence itself had moved across it. The feeling which had driven him over the wall rose up again now. He pulled himself to his feet and staggered forward, shouting into the sunlit darkness.

'Look, Roly, pack it in, can't you? I know you're...'

His foot struck stone. For an instant the world was suspended. Then the stone struck back, biting into his forehead. Even in the fragment of a second before he went reeling into the grass, he knew what it was that had tripped him. The gravestone. This had all happened before. But this time there was no hand to save him.

He hit the ground.

'Matt!'

The hand was on his shoulder, the arm round him.

'Matt! I'm sorry, Matt! I'm sorry!'

For a moment he felt too stunned to react. He let himself be held, understanding only that Roly was here, that it was all right again.

'Matt, are you OK? – Say you're OK, Matt!'

The hand was on his temples, stroking the hair away from his forehead. A bead of wetness feathered across his eyebrow, down the side of his nose.

'It's only a graze, Matt, honestly. Your mum'll fix it up OK. – Matt, say something, can't you?'

The memory of the past few minutes returned, bringing back the wrongness of things. He turned slowly to the voice beside him.

'You were here all the time, weren't you?'

For an instant the hand on his forehead froze. Matthew held his breath, waiting. But the voice gave no answer. He spoke again.

'You were here, weren't you? Just watching me. . . Why didn't you answer when I shouted? . . . You didn't want me to find you, did you?'

The fingers trembled across his temples again, and the voice came at last, broken and helpless.

'Look, Matt, haven't you got a hankie or something? It's bleeding. . .'

With a sudden rush of anger and misery Matthew wrenched the hand from his forehead, tightening his fingers round the wrist. 'Answer me, can't you! I asked you a question! You didn't want me to find you, did you? You knew we were waiting for you, didn't you? You knew why I was looking for you! And you weren't going to come! Were you? – *Were you?*'

'*No!*'

The word came like a cry of pain. Though Matthew had known already what the answer would be, it struck him speechless. For a long moment there was nothing, no sound and no movement. They sat there, face to face, without breathing. Then he heard his own voice again, choking with tears and fury.

'*Why?* What are you playing at?'

'Don't, Matt, please! I'm sorry!'

Matthew let go of his grip on the wrist, thrusting it violently from him. He scrambled to his feet.

'Who the hell do you think you're kidding?'

'Matt, I can't explain. I'm sorry, that's all!'

'Is that the only thing you can say? Go and say it to Mum then, she's the one you ought to be saying it to! She's the one who's been working herself half dead all day with cakes and trifles. She's even bought sherry, hasn't she! But I suppose that makes it better, doesn't it, I suppose it gives you a real kick knowing she's done all that when she can't afford it!'

'Please, Matt, *don't!*'

'I suppose it's one hell of a joke to muck around down here when you know she's up there waiting for you, just sitting and looking at it all. She's even bought serviettes so you wouldn't look down on her! She's even put her best dress on!'

'*Please!*'

'Who the hell do you think you are anyway? I suppose our food's not good enough for you or something! I suppose *we're* not bloody good enough for you! Is that it?'

Suddenly Roly was on his feet. His hand closed on Matthew's chest, bunching his T-shirt.

'Don't say that! Don't *ever* say that again!'

Matthew paused, breathing hard. Something in Roly had changed. The helpless sobbing had gone from his voice and there was a new note there now, hushed and tense. Not misery now, or even threat. It was a note of terror. '*Ever again, d'you hear?*'

There was a long moment of silence. In spite of his startlement, Matthew was the first to find his voice.

'What the hell are you on about?'

'*D'you hear?*'

With a brusque movement Matthew pushed away the hand that held him. He glared a frightened challenge at the emptiness before him.

'All right. If it's not true, prove it!'

Roly's voice came again, panting as he found his breath. 'Prove what?'

'Prove that you're not too good for us. Prove it for Mum's sake. There's still time. The tea's still there, isn't it? I can tell her you were delayed.' The terrified silence told him he'd won. 'Well? . . . Lost your tongue or something?'

When Roly finally answered, it was as if he'd collapsed.

'All right, Matt. If that's what you want.'

'It's not what *I* want, is it! I told you, it's for Mum!'

'OK.'

'Half an hour then. I'll go and get this blood washed off and prepare her, OK?'

'Yes.'

'And if you chicken out again, I'll. . .'

'I won't.' The footsteps moved off, and then paused once more. 'I've tried, Matt, I really have.' The voice trailed away into tears. It turned from him, and Roly had gone.

Fifteen

Matthew stood by the hedge at the bottom of the garden, staring out at the greyness which was his pathway. He could see it before him, without eyes. His feet had shown him its windings. Soon other feet would be on it, but the same windings would lead them to where he waited. This time, he knew, Roly would come.

A finger of wetness spidered down his face. He reached up, touching it. But the sticking-plaster was still in its place and the bleeding had stopped. His forehead was trickling with sweat. He shivered, cold in the sunlight.

Not long now.

He turned his head back towards the cottage and listened. The window was open but the kitchen was silent. In the sitting-room beyond, at the front, his mother was waiting. Faintly, when he strained his ears, he could hear the sounds of her waiting, her voice humming, clearing its throat, humming again, trying to find the tune. He drew a long breath and closed his eyes. It was all right again, for her at least it was all right. In spite of the lateness, in spite of the blood, she was happy again, because *he* was happy. . .

In every nerve of his body he could feel now the effort his 'happiness' had cost him. The memory of it returned like a nightmare. But she'd believed it. She'd believed his smiling and laughter and hadn't heard the sobbing inside him when she'd started smiling and laughing too. And his pretending wasn't over even now. In a few minutes the footsteps would come and the nightmare would start again.

He turned back to the waiting pathway.

A new thought clenched on his stomach. It wasn't just his mother he had to face now. It was Roly. After all that had happened down there in the churchyard, the bitterness and anger, they had to face each other again, speak to each other. They had to pretend to begin again, knowing there was no new beginning, knowing it was over. . . From deep inside him, four days of happiness welled up. They tightened on his throat, telling him what it was that he'd had, now that he'd lost it. It wasn't just friendship that he'd had, it was seeing. Roly had been his seeing. For four days he had shared his eyes. Now it was dark again, inside and out.

His fists closed on the hedge, fighting back tears. It couldn't be true, this afternoon couldn't have happened. . . But behind his eyes he was back in the churchyard and he knew that it *was* true, *had* happened.

He heard again the words that he'd spoken, and their echo pained him. But there was a deeper pain too, the pain of the answering echo, the words that Roly had spoken. Down there, he hadn't heard them. They had been too quiet and his own anger had been louder. But here, by the hedge, his anger was silent and Roly's words were clearer.

He stood for a moment, listening and hearing. *I can't explain. I'm sorry, that's all. . . I've tried, I really have. . .* He frowned suddenly, listening again and hearing for the first time what the words had told him. That he'd been wrong. It wasn't true that Roly had snubbed them, he hadn't stayed away out of spite. It wasn't spite in his words, it was something else, something that made no sense at all. It was misery. As if he'd wanted to come, but couldn't. As if his words had been a cry for understanding.

Matthew stared wildly at the emptiness before him, trying to answer the cry. But he knew only that he had no answer, that he understood nothing. A sob broke from him and he knuckled it back, biting on his fist.

Nothing about Roly made sense any more. He remembered the moments of happiness, when Roly had been glad to show him things and share them; and the moments of sadness, when the showing and sharing had stopped. And other moments too, the fear in the voice as they'd stood at the edge of the water, the unexplained hurry away from the room in the Hall. There was a rightness in Roly, and a wrongness. The pieces didn't fit. . . And yet there had to be a pattern in it all, there *had* to be. He must *think*. . .

But no thoughts came, only numbness. He felt suddenly more weary than he'd ever felt before. It was hopeless. His hand dropped limply to the hedge. He closed his eyes, not moving.

Somewhere far out, a small wind woke the rushes. He heard them sigh as it touched them. Then they slept again. He listened to their sleep, sharing it, unthinking. The time for thinking wasn't now, wasn't yet. Later perhaps. Later perhaps he'd be able to think better, understand better. He'd talk to someone. Ask someone. Ask Roly.

Roly. . .

A sound jolted at his stomach. He was suddenly awake, his whole body tensed and listening. It came again, sharper now, nearer. The sound of footsteps on gravel. A turmoil of feelings welled up in him, joy and fear. Nearing the final bend in the path now, rounding it. . . The footsteps faltered for an instant, then came on. With a cry he threw himself towards them.

'Roly!'

He clung to him, not caring any more, knowing only that he was here, that it was all right. The words tumbled from him.

'Roly, I'm sorry. I'm sorry what I said. It was my fault, I got it all wrong, that's all, I got in a state. But it's OK now, isn't it? We'll talk about it later, – after tea, when you've met Mum and everything. She's great now, dead excited about it – and she doesn't mind, honestly, about you being late or anything. She's waiting for us – she said to come round the front and have tea right away, then I can show you my room and you can stay as long as you like. We'll have a talk then, OK?'

He paused, breathless, grinning with the relief of having spoken. Roly answered quietly, through a throat too tight for speaking.

'OK, Matt.'

'And she doesn't know, I didn't tell her – you know, about down there, what happened or anything, so its OK. And I *am* sorry, Roly, honestly I am.'

'Me too.'

'Let's forget it for a bit then, OK? We can sort it all out later when we're on our own. . .' He faltered for an instant, biting his lip. 'I'd really like to, Roly, more than anything. Sort things out a bit, I mean. There're things I want to tell you, and . . . and ask you. Things I don't really get.' Beneath his hand, Roly's arm tautened. 'OK?'

When Roly answered, the same tautness was in his voice.

'OK. Let's go now, shall we?'

Matthew hesitated again, wondering what expression was in the eyes, and whether they were meeting his own. He forced himself to go on, knowing that he had to.

'It'll be all right, Roly, you'll see. We'll talk about things and they'll be all right. I want to straighten things out a bit before. . . before I go home. We can, can't we?'

'Oh, yes.' Matthew listened, not knowing what he'd heard in the voice, whether fear or sadness or laughter. 'Come on, Matt, let's go. Please.'

Matthew took a deep breath and smiled. 'OK, Roly.'

Together they went up through the garden, round the side of the cottage, not speaking. The front door was open. For an instant Roly hung back. Matthew turned, grinning. He spoke in a whisper.

'Don't worry, Roly. Soon be over now.'

'Yes.'

With his hand on his sleeve, Matthew led him quietly into the hallway and along to the sitting-room door. Then he pushed him gently inside. His voice rang out, loud in the stillness.

'Hi, Mum, guess who's come to tea!'

He heard her jump slightly. The magazine closed and slid to the floor as she turned towards the door and stood up.

'Oh how lovely! I didn't hear you com. . .'

Her voice wavered. In the doorway, Matthew grinned again.

'Sorry, we thought we'd surprise you. This is Roly, Mum. . . – Mum?'

His mother hadn't moved. She stood by the sofa in silence. When her voice came, it held an attempt at laughter.

'Well bring him in, Matt. Don't be silly.'

For a moment her words hung in the air without meaning. Then he stepped forward from the doorway towards her.

'It's Roly, Mum.'

The silence came again, senseless and empty. He stared into it, feeling his grin tremble. 'Mum?'

Her dress rustled forward, uncertain. Then passed him, towards the doorway. It paused and turned back. Her voice came again, trying to smile at a joke.

'Stop being silly, love.'

'What d'you mean?'

'Where is he?'

The words were crazy. He looked at the greyness before him, suddenly afraid.

'Roly?'

There was no answer.

'Matt, please, this is daft. Where is he?'

'Roly!'

He stepped across the room. A chair struck at his foot and slid away, scraping on tiles.

'Matt, stop it.'

'Roly!!'

'Stop it, Matt!'

He swung towards her.

'What's up with you, Mum? He's here! He came in with

me! – Roly!'

'He's not here, Matt, you know he's not. Now stop it.'

For a wild moment he looked at the place where he knew Roly had been standing when he'd let go of his sleeve, then back towards his mother. He stared from one emptiness to the other.

'Roly? . . . Mum? . . . Speak for God's sake!'

'Matt! Don't!'

She moved towards him. Her hands gripped his shoulders.

'What's going on, Mum? Speak to him!'

'Stop it!'

His breath choked in his throat. His voice came through it, angry and frightened.

'Pack it in, can't you! It's not fair! What the hell are you both playing at? Speak to each other, damn you!'

'*Stop it!*'

Her hand struck out and sang across his ear. She staggered back, gasping in horror at what she'd done. For a moment that seemed endless they stood there frozen, face to face. Then he pushed past her towards the door.

'Where are you going, Matt?'

'Out! I want to be on my own!'

'But where?'

'Out!!'

He heard her following, felt her hand on his shoulder.

'Matt, please! Tell me where you're going!'

'Where d'you think! I'm blind, remember? There's only one place I *can* go on my own, isn't there, in the whole bloody world!'

He shook himself free and stumbled out through the hallway, slamming the door on her sobs.

'Roly!'

His cry rang out into emptiness, echoing away beyond the church.

'Roly!!'

The emptiness took up the name again, spinning it away farther and farther. He listened to its departing echo, out across the land to seaward. Then it was only the rushes again, and he knew that it had gone from him.

He stood there, staring into the grey sunlight, not moving, knowing only that it was over. Roly had left him, and the time for understanding was past.

Suddenly the stillness was torn apart. For an instant his heart stopped beating. He fell back from the wall and listened. A grating of wood on stone. Then another sound tapped out, a sound he knew well. A sob of relief broke from him. The door of the church had opened. Footsteps were in the porch.

One last desperate hope threw him forward.

'Mr Chapman?'

There was a startled pause, then a voice shouted towards him.

'Matthew is it?'

He scrambled up onto the wall and dropped down on the other side. The footsteps were coming towards him. It was all right. It could still be all right. He fought back the panting in his chest and stood up, gritting his teeth to keep his voice steady.

'Mr Chapman, have you seen Roly?'

'Who?'

'Roly. Roland Johnson.'

'Oh, Roland.' His voice crowed suddenly, bright with a dawning idea. 'Ah, it was *you* then, was it? I *said* there was somebody yelling but Annie wouldn't have it – that's Mrs Chapman, I mean. We've been giving the church a bit of a going-over, ready for Sunday. We were up the other end though so it was hard to be sure, but I reckoned I ought to come and have a look just the same, to be on the safe side in case anybody was after us. But it was Roland you were wanting, was it?'

'Yes. Have you seen him?'

'Well now. . .' He scratched, thinking. Matthew stood and waited. A wave of desperation rose up in him.

'Please, Mr Chapman, it's important.'

'I was just thinking. I did see him, now I recall.'

'Lately?'

'Fairly lately it must've been, I reckon.'

'Can you remember exactly?'

'Oh, as for exactly, no, I don't reckon I could put an exact day on it or anything.'

'*Day?* But it's *today* I mean, *now,* in the past few minutes, down here in the churchyard!'

Mr Chapman paused for a moment, letting the idea take root. Then he chuckled.

'Oh, it's *today* you're meaning, is it? No, I haven't seen him today. Not to remember, I haven't.'

With a suddenness he couldn't control, Matthew's desperation burst from him. He threw himself forward, clutching at Mr Chapman's arm.

'I've got to see him, Mr Chapman, I've got to find him. *I've got to!*'

There was a surprised silence. The voice cleared its throat and came again, puzzled and concerned.

'Something amiss, is there? Something happened?'

'No it's not that. I can't explain, it's just important, that's all. I've got to tell him something, ask him something, before I go home.'

'Well I'd like to help, but I don't see what. . .'

'Take me to him!. . . Please!'

'But I've told you, I would if I could, willing, but I haven't seen him. I don't know where he is.'

'But you know where he lives, don't you? You said so. The big house at the end of the village. It won't take long, it's not far, is it?'

'Oh, well as to that. . .'

‘Mr Chapman, *please!* I haven’t got anybody else I can ask. And I can’t go on my own. I can’t really get about like I told you, that was all showing off. I can’t even get round the churchyard. You’ve *got* to help me, it’s my last chance!’

He came to a breathless halt, biting back tears. He waited. Then relief swept through him.

‘All right, Matthew, don’t upset yourself, lad. Of course I’ll take you if that’s what you’re wanting. Now come on, buck up a bit, it’s all right now.’

‘Thanks, Mr Chapman, I. . .’

A sob caught at his throat and he faltered.

‘I know what you’re meaning so you save your breath for the walking. – I’ll just give Mrs Chapman a shout and let her know where we’re heading. – Annie!’ His voice echoed away towards the church. ‘Annie!’

Matthew turned away, wiping his sleeve across his face. It was going to be all right. He’d talk to Roly, find out what had happened, sort things out. . .

Footsteps sounded in the church porch.

‘Oh Annie. It *was* somebody shouting, like I said – young Matthew here. He was after a friend of his, to have a word with before he goes home tomorrow. So I’m going to walk him down there. I’ll only be a few minutes.’

‘That’s all right. Who is it then?’

‘Roland Johnson, from down the village.’

The short silence which followed Mr Chapman’s words was broken by a chuckle from the porch. The sound of it froze Matthew to the spot. With a sudden feeling of dread, he waited for her to go on.

‘You’ll have to get a move on then, if you’re reckoning on being back in a few minutes. It’s a fair old step to Devon.’

‘What’re you going on about, Annie?’

‘Devon. That’s where the Johnsons are. In Devon on holiday.’

Matthew swung round, staring wildly across to the church.

'They can't be, Mrs Chapman!'

'Oh they are. They're in Devon all right. Mrs Carter told me and she ought to know. She's next door and keeps an eye on things when they're away.'

'But they can't *all*'ve gone! Not Roly as well!'

'They have, dear, the whole lot of them.'

'But perhaps they've decided not to! Perhaps they're waiting till tomorrow!'

'No, they've gone all right. Mrs Carter told me.'

'But when did she tell you?'

'When I was having a cup of tea with her – yesterday, that was.'

'*Yesterday!* But she can't have! They can't have gone before yesterday!'

'I'm afraid they did, dear, there's no changing the fact. They left on Wednesday.'

Sixteen

Mrs Weaver's voice smiled.

'Let them come, Matthew, let the tears come if they want to or they'll just go on hurting and hurting inside. Stop being brave, stop thinking you'll upset me. I'm just a hand to hold on to, that's all, while you cry.'

And holding on to her hand, he cried. He cried until there was no more crying left inside him, kneeling by her chair. And slowly the sobbing grew quiet and the hurting ebbed from him, in tears that tasted like the sea.

Her hand freed itself gently and lifted his face towards her.

'There, that's the worst of it over. At least you'll be able to find your voice a bit now, won't you, and tell me what's the matter? . . . What's happened, Matthew? Was it so very bad?'

'I don't know. I don't know anything any more. I just want you to help me.'

'But how can I help you if you won't tell me what's wrong? There must be something I can do, mustn't there, or you wouldn't have come.'

He bit his lip, knowing why he'd come, not knowing how to tell her.

'Yes.'

'Then tell me.'

He knelt there, trying to find the words and the courage to speak them. Then he froze. Another voice had come, calling from the adjoining garden. 'Mrs Weaver?'

She hoisted herself up with her hand on his shoulder and limped away to the window. The voice came again, quieter now, with an edge of strain.

'Did I see Matthew come round, Mrs Weaver, a few minutes back?'

'Yes, don't worry, Mrs Mason, he's here.' He heard her turn back towards him and knew she was reading his face. He held his breath. Then relief swept through him. 'He's going to stay a while, if that's all right.'

The voice outside hesitated. 'Yes. . . yes, of course. Can you tell him I've got a bit of a headache, I'm going to have a lie-down upstairs. I've left him his tea on the kitchen table when he's ready, with a glass of milk. And. . . and can you ask him to promise to come straight back home when he leaves you?'

'Of course, Mrs Mason. I'll watch him round myself.'

'Thank you. And. . .' The voice faltered again. 'And I'd like him to pop in and see me upstairs, before he goes to bed. To say goodnight.'

He knew that Mrs Weaver turned again towards him, though she didn't speak. He looked away, feeling suddenly wretched. Her voice answered gently through the open window.

'He promises, Mrs Mason. He won't forget.'

And it was over. The voice outside had left them and Mrs Weaver was back, holding his hand in hers as he knelt by her chair.

'It was a row, Matthew, wasn't it? You've had a row with your mum?'

'Yes.'

'Do you want to talk about it? Do you want to tell me about it?'

He stared emptily at the floor, knowing he had to speak.

'It's not that, Mrs Weaver. Or at least that's sort of part of it. But it's not just the row, it's other things. This week and everything.'

'What about this week, Matthew? Haven't you enjoyed it here?'

'Oh yes, it's been great. It's been about the greatest thing that's ever happened to me. But. . .'

'But what?'

'Well, there've been things I haven't sort of got straight, things I want to know. Things about Malham. They've been on my mind.'

'What things? What on earth can have been troubling you about Malham?'

He turned his face slowly towards her, tightening his grip on her hand.

'Mrs Weaver, if I ask you something about Malham, something I want to know more than anything, will you promise to tell me?'

'Well of course, if I can.'

'You promise?'

'Of course I promise.'

He took a deep breath.

'I want you to tell me about the Hall, Mrs Weaver. I want to know what happened to the Latimers.'

Beneath his own, her hand tautened. There was a long silence. When she spoke, there was pain in her voice.

'But why, Matthew? What difference can it make now? It was all so long ago.'

'I can't explain. I don't even know whether it'll make any difference or not. I just want to find out, that's all. Mrs Weaver, you promised!'

'I know. I know I did. Don't upset yourself again.' Her voice trailed away for a moment. 'But there seems no sense in it, Matthew, dragging it all back up now.'

'But all what? That's what I want to find out! That's what's been worrying me! *Why* don't you want to tell me?'

'Oh I don't know. Because it's a sad story, I suppose. Because there's enough sadness in the world already, without raking up all the sadness of the past. And what importance can it have now?'

'I don't *know*, I told you. Perhaps it's not important at all, but I've just got to find out. I can't explain. I would if I could, but I'm not even sure myself. Please, Mrs Weaver,

I've *got* to know. It can't make any difference me knowing, can it? I go home tomorrow.' A sob caught at his throat and he bit it back. 'It might just help, that's all. – I can't go home without knowing. It's been sort of part of it all, part of this week and Malham and everything. . . *Please*.'

The silence lengthened. In the corner, the clock ticked out the seconds of it. Then with a deep whirring it struck seven times across the stillness. It was as if a decision had been reached. Mrs Weaver stirred and sighed.

'All right, Matthew. If you think it'll help. If it'll put your mind at rest.'

He closed his eyes. The strain went from his body. Whatever was coming now, whatever he was going to hear, at least it would be something. The quietness settled, listening.

'It's so difficult, Matthew, after all these years. I hardly know where to begin.'

'Begin where your grandmother did, when she used to tell you. Tell it me just like she did.'

'That was a long time ago, my dear.'

'But you do remember, don't you?'

'Oh yes. I remember.'

He took her hand in his, feeling its oldness, and she smiled, remembering. And he knew that once, long ago, she had knelt by the chair, as he was kneeling, and had held another hand, as old as hers was now.

She spoke.

'It was in the days of the last Latimers, Edward Latimer and his wife. A fine young man, Edward was, and brave too – his parents had died early on in his life, within a few hours of each other, it was said. Diphtheria or some such thing it was, and no cure to be had in those times. Edward couldn't have been much more than twenty when it happened, and still at the university. He'd known he'd inherit one day, of course, as the only child of the family. But it must have been a terrible shock to him, to find it happening so soon.

'I've often wondered what it must have been like for him, coming back here from Oxford with his parents just passed away, to take charge of everything on his own and no brothers and sisters to help him. There was the funeral to arrange, and the servants upset, and the Hall and estate to see to – and the village as well, with him being squire now his father was dead. People must have shaken their heads then, and thought the grand old days of the Latimers were over and done with. But he proved them all wrong. He never let the sadness take hold or the old times die. It was as if he'd sworn to himself that he'd do it for *her* sake, the girl he would bring here to marry. And when he was ready, he brought her.

'Lucy, her name was, and the loveliest creature you could ever imagine. Some say there was never her equal at the Hall before, in all the years it had stood there. Oh there was happiness then all right. It was as if she'd brought it with her, as her gift to him. The old place was alive again, with the carriages arriving and the champagne flowing, and the chandelier burning all night in the hallway for the dancing that went on till dawn. They were generous and no mistake, were the Latimers, with their friends and their servants alike.'

Matthew smiled, remembering the scene below him as he'd closed his eyes and looked through the bars of the gallery. He spoke softly, as if afraid to startle her.

'Were there children, Mrs Weaver?'

But she'd drifted from him now. She went on as if she'd heard his question from far away, like one of her own memories.

'And in all that happiness there was only one shadow, one gift she didn't bring. I don't know any more how many years they hoped and waited. But it was only when their hope had gone from them that their waiting was at last rewarded. It was a son.'

She fell silent for a moment, and in her silence Matthew

heard the joy of the past.

'If there was ever a child born to more happiness than that one, he'd be hard to imagine. He had everything he could have asked for, and more. There were never clothes seen like it, before or since. And toys. . . well, he couldn't have played with all of them if he'd tried. His mother worshipped him, took care of him herself from the start, and wouldn't let another soul near him but his father. Edward was the same, worshipped the ground he walked on, and it was easy to see why – the lad had all his mother's beauty, the same black hair and paleness and deep dark eyes. Yes, it was worship all right and no mistake, his name was on their lips from morning till night. . .'

She drifted again. Hardly breathing, Matthew spoke, drawing her back towards him.

'It was Rupert, Mrs Weaver, wasn't it? His name was Rupert.'

'Yes. Rupert. And they wouldn't see that what they were doing was wrong, that too much love can be wrong. They couldn't see it even when the signs were there for all to see. And every servant up there at the Hall did see them, the signs, but nobody could speak them aloud. Servants can't meddle with worship like that, and keep their jobs. And so they kept silent and watched it happen. They watched him get more and more spoilt, demanding more and more toys – and getting them too. He'd play with them for an hour then throw them from him, bored with them, as he was bored with all the rest. And he treated people the same. He treated the servants as he treated his toys, and no Latimer before him had ever done that. And he was a strange one in other ways too, was Rupert. . .'

'Strange?'

'Oh yes. He was one for his own thoughts all right, never chatting or laughing like other boys his age. He didn't *know* any other boys his age, that was part of the trouble. An only child, twelve years old and growing to a man, with none but his own company, it's all wrong. And never going out, either, just keeping himself to himself and never going out, with Malham as lovely as it is. Just keeping to his room.'

'Was it. . . was it a nice room, Mrs Weaver?'

'Oh, the best of course. Right at the top, with a view any other lad would've given his right arm for, a view of the creeks and sea. But not Rupert. He never even noticed it, more likely than not. How could he, with his curtains drawn all day? He didn't notice it at all, until. . .'

'Until? Until what?'

He knew that she was smiling now, but the smile was sad.

'Until Tom came.' He waited, not moving. She spoke again, as if answering her own thoughts. 'Yes. Tom came. And if ever there were two creatures more different, they'd be hard to find. There never was anyone more cheerful and full of life than Tom was. He loved everything, the village and the creeks and the sea, and was never indoors except to sleep. He hardly knew the inside of the cottage by daylight, I shouldn't think, in all the weeks he was here.'

'Cottage? . . . Which cottage?'

'Next door. That's where they lived, and his mother could hardly believe how lucky she'd been to get a place like that to live in. They were different times then, for servants.'

'Did she come to be a servant at the Hall?'

'Yes, she came as the cook, and Tom did odd jobs round the garden. He worked hard too, when he wasn't chasing off to the creeks. And then the two lads met. . .'

'What happened, Mrs Weaver?'

'The one thing nobody would've thought or believed. They became friends. . . And yet perhaps it's not so difficult to understand after all. Perhaps it was like a new world to both of them. . .

'Tom hadn't had anything from the day he was born and now here he was suddenly, invited inside the Hall - not just in the servants' quarters but in the Hall itself, where people like him never went. And he was shown things he'd never even dreamed of seeing. Think what the toys and games and books were like for someone who'd never even *seen* a proper toy before. And think what it was like to be treated as a special guest by the master and mistress of the house, because Rupert insisted on it, and to be given free entry up the main staircase and even to the private top floor, because Rupert insisted on that too. And then there were no more gardening jobs, because Rupert wouldn't allow it. Oh it's not so difficult to understand what happened, why Tom began to share in the worship of Rupert. So they spent every minute of the day together, inside the Hall and out. . .'

Again she paused, and seemed to answer an unspoken question.

'Yes, outside too. Because that was the gift that Tom could give Rupert in return. He could show him a new world too. And Rupert went with him and saw it, for the first time in his life. The creeks and the saltings and the sea. They shared the magic of it together. Rupert would wait for him, every morning in the hallway, wait for him to come running across the garden, to fetch him. . .

'And all this time the folk up at the Hall were watching what was happening, hoping that it was a new beginning, but secretly dreading that the end was already in sight.'

And Matthew felt the same dread, not knowing what he dreaded. The last shadow of a smile had gone from the voice beside him, leaving nothing but sadness.

'It came, as it had to. For Tom, the friendship was the only thing in his life, it was part of him now. But for Rupert. . . For Rupert, it was like everything else – like a new toy. He'd asked for it and been given it and played with it for a while, and now it had begun to bore him. So he threw it away.'

There was a long silence. The clock ticked heavily, tightening minute by minute towards the chime.

'There's more, Mrs Weaver, isn't there.'

Her voice grew quieter.

'Not much more now. Only two days more.'

A shiver walked up Matthew's spine, numbing him.

'Rupert behaved as he'd always done, spoilt and spiteful. He forbade Tom to come near him again, and the more Tom tried the more Rupert's anger grew. He forbade him to enter any part of the Hall but the servants' quarters, told him he'd have his mother sacked if he did. And so Tom had to stay away. He stayed away for two days. The servants saw the misery in him but there was nothing they could do. And it was the servants who saw the end of it too, from the hallway. They saw his final wretched attempt to make it up with Rupert. . .'

She paused, seeing it again as her grandmother had shown it to her.

'It was late on the last evening, when the Latimer parents were out. The servants saw the front door open and Tom come in, rushing across the hallway to the main staircase. They tried to call him back, but he was crying too much to hear. He just went on, racing up to the first gallery, then the second. They heard his footsteps thudding along the final corridor, and his hammering on Rupert's door. Then the door opened and there was nothing, until . . . until the row broke out. It was the worst thing they'd ever heard, Tom sobbing and Rupert screaming and cursing. For a minute they were too frightened to move, and by the time they did it was over. Footsteps were crashing down the staircase again towards them. But it wasn't Tom. It was Rupert. They said the sight of him froze them, they'd never seen anger like it on any face before. His voice screamed out at them as he pushed past them, cursing them out of his way and ordering them to stop Tom coming after him. But there was nothing they could do. Tom's footsteps came almost at once, and they couldn't hold him. With his face streaming with tears he flung himself out of the front door into the darkness, following Rupert they didn't know where. It was only later that they knew.'

Their hands were still joined, but too cold for feeling. The silence was terrible. Matthew heard his own voice speaking, as if from a great distance.

'It was to the sea, wasn't it. They went to the sea.'

'Out across the creeks and along the dyke, Rupert rushing headlong away and Tom following. Out to the sea. What happened when they got there, nobody knows.'

Matthew wasn't sure if he spoke again. Mrs Weaver seemed to answer, in words hardly loud enough for hearing. But when they came, they struck him like a blow.

'Ah yes, their bodies were found. Tom's had gone out with the tide, far out. But Rupert's was thrown back to shore, stranded when the tide turned and left it. They found it next day, lying among the shells.'

The voice fell silent. From somewhere far away, the clock struck the half hour. Mrs Weaver stirred and reached out. Grey lamplight filled the room.

'There, Matthew. Now you know.'

'Yes.' His hand slipped limply from hers.

'Oh my dear, it's upset you as I knew it would. I shouldn't have told you.'

'It's all right.' He paused for a few seconds, trying to steady his voice. 'What happened to the Latimers? The parents?'

'Oh, they left the Hall. The shock was too much for them, I suppose, and they died soon after. – Come on, my dear, you look quite dazed with it all. And you're so cold!' She rubbed his hand gently between her own. 'You must be getting back soon, to see your mum. She'll be waiting. And life goes on in spite of old stories. That's all it is, an old story. – Is it what you wanted to know, at least? Are you satisfied now?'

'Yes. . .' He hesitated, holding his breath. Then his words rushed out. 'Mrs Weaver, why did you jump like that in the hallway next door – you know, when we first met?'

'Oh Matthew. . .'

'Please, you can tell me now, can't you? You've told me everything else.'

She paused for a moment, then seemed to reach a decision, as if she knew she had come too far to turn back.

'All right, my dear, but then it's finished. Not another word after that. It sounds sillier now than ever, but I'll tell you if you make *me* a promise.'

'What promise?'

'That you'll tell me I'm just a muddled old woman, and won't let it upset you. Do you promise?'

'Yes.'

She laughed, and hoisted herself from her chair. He heard her limp away to the other end of the room and draw something heavy from a cupboard. Pages turned. He held his breath, waiting.

'It's a photograph album, Matthew, that's all. It belonged to my grandmother. There's a photograph in it I've known ever since I was a girl.'

The pages fell silent. He felt her looking towards him. With a strange feeling of numbness, he stood up and fumbled his way across to her side.

'What is it, Mrs Weaver? Tell me.'

'It's faded now, but the faces are still there. It was taken in the hallway of the cottage you're staying in.'

Trembling, he reached out and touched the photograph, wondering what it would tell him. Her voice spoke again.

'I know it's silly, Matthew, but I remembered it when I saw you there, standing by the door like he is.'

'Like who is?'

'Like Tom. You're so alike, it startled me. It's a picture of Tom and Rupert.'

'How do you know? How do you know it's Tom and Rupert?'

'It says so on the back.' He heard her draw out the photograph from the corners that held it, turning it over to the light. 'The ink's faint now. I suppose it was Rupert who wrote it, because Rupert must've been the one who had it taken. He's dated it August 1887, and there're just the two names. Tom and Roly.'

For an instant the world seemed to spin. He clutched at the cupboard to stop himself falling.

'What? What did you say?'

'It's just the date and the names, so it must be Tom and Rupert.'

'But that's not what you said. Not Rupert. You said something else. You said another name.'

'Yes. But it's Rupert all right. It's just what Tom used to call him, that's all, a sort of nickname, I suppose, from his initials. Rupert Oliver Latimer. R.O.L. – Roly.'

Seventeen

He stood on the upper landing, outside the door to his mother's bedroom. He could hear the sound of her breathing, less calm than his own. His calmness surprised him. He wondered what feeling was inside him. No feeling at all, perhaps, only the numbness of shock. Or the calmness of certainty. Not the certainty of final understanding, not yet. But the certainty that he now knew the way he must follow, to reach the ending.

He pressed the latch gently and went in.

His mother started slightly, propping herself up against pillows. 'Matt?' Her voice winced, and she sank back. He stepped forward to her bed and felt her take his hand. 'I must've dozed off a bit, you made me jump.'

'Sorry.'

'That's all right, I'm glad you popped in. Have you had your tea?'

'Yes, a bit.'

'Were you with Mrs Weaver long?'

'Not really. It's about quarter past eight, I think.' Her hand was heavy and limp. He could feel the throbbing of its pulse, and knew that the same throbbing was in her head. 'Do you want an aspirin, Mum?'

'I've had a couple already and it's still thumping fit to burst. It'll be all right in the morning, when I've had a bit of sleep.' She paused for a moment, then the pillow sighed as she turned her face towards him. 'I can't say much, love. I just wanted to tell you I'm sorry. About what happened.'

'Yes. So am I.'

'I know you only did it because you were all upset about him not coming and everything. But you shouldn't have, Matt, it didn't make things any better.'

'No.'

'I'm just sorry I didn't try and understand a bit more. I shouldn't have done what I did, I didn't mean it.'

'I know.'

'I was in a state too, that's all. But it's OK now, isn't it? We're still the same, you and me?'

'Yes.'

He answered the faint squeeze of her hand, and it fell back beside her.

'You go and get to bed then, we've got a big day tomorrow. You'll be able to manage on your own, won't you? You know where everything is?'

'Yes, that's all right.'

'Night night then, Matt. God bless.'

'And you, Mum.'

'It'll be all behind us by the morning, won't it?'

'Yes.'

He closed the door gently after him and went to his room. For a few seconds he stood there, listening. But there was no movement from beyond the wall. She was already asleep.

He walked across to his bed and lay down without undressing. Then he switched off the lamp.

He reached out again to the clock. Its fingers touched his own. Ten past eleven. Still twenty minutes until the time he'd decided on.

He lay back. With the same strange calmness he'd felt ever since leaving Mrs Weaver, he continued to stare up into the darkness, as if checking and rechecking a pattern he saw there. He nodded to himself. It was almost complete.

It was true then. What Roly had said down by the creeks was true.

So you do believe it, Roly? – That people might be able to come back?

Of course. Don't you?

Roly had known. He'd known from the beginning that

Tom had come back. And Matthew knew now, too. He'd been here before, and had at last returned. His eyes hadn't tricked him. The things he'd seen had been real. He'd seen them as Tom had once seen them. The rows of windows, bright in the darkness, as Tom had first seen them one night long ago, when he and his mother had come up the driveway to begin their new life at the Hall. *She came as the cook...* He remembered the silence which had followed his own words to Roly, two days ago on the beach.

Where does she work, Matt?
In London, in a canteen. She's a cook.

Then the other images returned, and his own footsteps racing across them: the Hall garden in sunlight, the top corridor, the creeks. But Mrs Weaver's voice echoed there too now, giving them meaning.

Rupert would wait for Tom, every morning in the hallway, wait for him to come running across the garden to fetch him...

They heard Tom's footsteps thudding along the final corridor, and his hammering on Rupert's door...

Out across the creeks and along the dyke, Rupert rushing headlong away and Tom following. Out to the sea...

Matthew stirred and raised his hand towards the bedside table. Twenty past eleven. He sank quietly back against the pillow, his eyes still open to the darkness of the room. The same darkness that Tom had once seen perhaps, the same room.

He wondered if the idea frightened him, but he wasn't sure. He felt no less real than he'd ever done, no less Matthew. Nothing had changed. And he was as real to other people as he was to himself, they called him by name, could *see* his reality with their own eyes. Whereas Roly...

His hands tightened slightly on the blanket.

Even now he could hardly believe what today had told him. But the pattern was too clear for doubting. The truth about Roly had locked the pieces together. It had been the key. Every moment they had spent together fitted into place now, from the need for the game at the beginning to the terror of the tea at the end.

I'll teach you my game if you like, Matt... we'll try and get through the whole walk without being spotted...

He's not here, Matt, you know he's not!...

And he understood too that in all these things Roland Johnson had played no part at all.

Roly? Oh Roland Johnson that'll be, he's the only Roland round here...

Mr Chapman hadn't known he was wrong, couldn't have known. Neither he nor anyone else in Malham who had eyes to see could have known that another Roly was moving among them, as invisible as a ghost.

Matthew stumbled on the word and for the first time a tremor of feeling awoke in him. But he knew that it wasn't a feeling of fear. For him at least, for him of all the people who could have come back here, the truth made no difference, the unseen held no fear. To him alone, Roly was real. He didn't need eyes to see him. The tremor came again, laughter and tears. Everything that had ever happened seemed to have been working out its hidden purpose and leading to this moment of time. He'd returned, and Roly had been able to come to him bringing no terrors, only a silent cry for help.

What help he could give and what the sadness in the voice had been trying to tell him, he didn't know, any more than he knew why he had come back in this way, living and real, while Roly had remained here always, like a restless spirit. But he knew now the path which would lead to the answer. He knew where Roly would be.

Reaching out again he touched the clock, and his fingers showed him the time as five days ago they had shown him the words on the gravestone.

Rupert Oliver Latimer. Died August 29th, 1887.

He smiled, biting back tears. In half an hour from now, the century would come full circle. It was one hundred years ago tonight.

He left his bed quietly and eased the door open. His mother was breathing evenly and his footsteps didn't disturb her. When he reached the hallway he waited again for a moment, listening. But nothing stirred.

He lifted the latch and stepped out into the darkness. The front door closed behind him.

Eighteen

The churchyard slept, and his whisper didn't wake it.

'Roly?'

Crouched on top of the wall he listened, knowing there would be no answer, expecting none. The village and estate lay silent. Daylight sounds had drained away, outward from the land, and left it empty. It wasn't here that he would find him now.

He turned his head.

Somewhere out there, beyond the stillness, a wind walked across the rushes, along the creeks and seaward. For a moment his ears followed its movement. He remained where he was, poised between his pathway and the waiting churchyard. He listened again, holding his breath. A second wind stirred, crossing the marshes, chasing the shadow of the first. Then both were gone, lost beyond the dunes, and there was only silence.

A pang of alarm shot through him, like a fear that he'd somehow delayed too long. He bit it back, knowing he must be calm, mustn't rush things. There was still time, plenty of time, it couldn't be more than a few minutes since he'd left the cottage. . .

Suddenly he froze. From far along the coast a sound had struck out like a warning, punching a hole in the stillness. Then another followed, and another. He clung to the top of the wall, not daring to believe what he was hearing. He couldn't have been waiting here so long, it couldn't be Saturday yet. . . Motionless, he counted the chimes. Ten. Eleven. And the twelfth stroke echoed towards him. With a cry he flung himself against it, into the churchyard.

He scrambled to his feet and moved forward, arms

outstretched. A gravestone reached out, rough against his fingers, and he knew that it was Rupert's. Panic caught at his stomach and he veered away, fumbling at the darkness, awaking other gravestones from their sleep. They jostled against him, catching at his feet and shoulders, spinning him off course. He paused for a moment, breathless, shrinking from their silent presence, not knowing any longer where the church was, or the street. Then tyres swished light across the blackness from behind him, yellow-grey, and thrummed away along the coast. He swung round, clenching his teeth to keep his bearings steady. Straight ahead now, and he would reach the wall and gateway. More gravestones lurched across his path. He held his course against them, steering round them with his toes and fingers towards the tarmac where the car had passed. Then nettles came, feathering pain along his hands, hot and cold. But he knew that he was close now, the wall was near.

It met him and turned him sharply to the right. He quickened his pace, letting it guide him, skimming his palms along its roughness until it fell away abruptly and left him in the gateway. He paused again, listening. The thumping in his ears slowed down, and the silence returned. Its emptiness frightened him suddenly. For the first time it told him what it was that he was doing. Clinging to the bars of the gate for support, he strained his ears out beyond the roadway. But there was nothing, not a breath of movement to lead him. He fought down rising panic, trying to recall Roly's words when first they'd hidden here together. *Three steps down, across the road, and the track's dead opposite. It's rough tarmac for about a hundred yards, and sharp left for another hundred or so. Then we're on the footpath out through the rushes. . .* He remembered the hand on his sleeve, guiding him as he ran. The memory choked him. *Just let yourself go and run like the wind. And Matt – I won't let you hurt yourself, I promise. You can trust me, can't you?* Sudden tears stung at his eyes and cheeks. He pressed his face against his hands on the gateway, knowing now what he'd lost. It was hopeless. Roly had gone beyond his reach. Without him, he was blind.

Then the world slipped away and nothing remained but the sharp wetness of rust on his eyes and fingers, and his own voice crying out a name. He heard it as if from an endless distance, over and over, like an echo. But there was no answering echo, only the slow silence again as his sobbing grew quiet. He lifted his face from the bars, raising his sleeve to wipe away tears. But even before it reached his cheeks, it froze.

His eyes stared wildly across it, as if shielding themselves from what lay beyond. Then slowly his arm fell away. But his eyes didn't move. They gazed unblinking at the darkness, and knew it was no longer the same. Shadows were in it, shadows of shadows, real and unreal like shapes in a mist. Things half known, forming and fading, caught in the twilight that moves between blindness and seeing, between present and past. Shadows of houses and emptier shadows of tarmac, the ghost of a path leading away into night. For a moment he stood there, as if afraid that the slightest motion might take it from him. Then he dragged the gate open and flung himself forward, across the roadway and into the track.

He ran, not knowing from second to second if his feet were showing him the path, or his eyes, hardly knowing any longer who he was. With every step the greyness changed and shifted, gathering into phantom shapes of grass and bushes, then dissolving again into mist. He swung aside from the tarmac and the silence was suddenly loud with rushes as his legs awoke them. Again the greyness changed and divided, light and dark, and he knew that the creeks were near now, with their masts against the sky. He threw himself on faster and the masts came closer, sweeping towards him on the rushes. Then the rushes were silent and the boats lay before him, stranded in mud where the tide had left them.

He paused, fighting for breath.

For an instant the darkness returned, blind and unbroken, then shifted once more, gathering itself in to its centre and detaching itself from the night. Motionless, he watched it, knowing already what form it was taking. Clearer now, so clear that even its shadows were appearing, shadows of stones and grasses and the steps of a rising pathway. The dyke. He fixed it with his eyes, holding it steady. Then, without warning, one of the shadows on it moved.

A cry choked in his throat, and his feet flung him forward. But the dyke was already melting, swimming away from him in streaks of light and darkness. He swept his sleeve across his eyes as he ran and for a moment the figure reappeared, climbing away from him up the steep slope and seaward.

'Roly!'

Desperation seized him and he drove himself on faster, stumbling up the pathway to the top of the dyke.

'Roly! *Stop!*'

But the footsteps were tearing away.

He followed, half seeing, half blinded, and knew that his blindness was only the blindness of tears. The path curved northward and he let it take him. Far ahead, darkness on darkness, the dunes were rising. Higher now and nearer as the dyke swooped down to the saltings. He swooped down with it, headlong into grass. When he looked again, Roly, and everything, had vanished.

'Roly! *Please!*'

His cry returned to him unanswered, echoing back from walls of dyke and dune. He scrambled forward, unseeing. His hands and knees met sand, firm and wet where the tide had touched it as it had swept its way down from the creeks. He crouched there, listening. No footsteps broke the stillness. Nothing moved. He turned his head slowly. Behind him the rushes lay silent, with no wind to wake them. But somewhere, faintly, he could still hear their whisper. He listened again, trying to trace it. Not behind him but before him, where no rushes grew. His panic tightened. All sense of direction had left him.

Then a memory stirred, an echo of the voice at his side when they'd stood by the creeks, when he'd asked where the rushes ended. *They don't. You can't see them any more once you've crossed the dunes, but they're still there. You can still hear their voices, out in the sea.* And he knew. It wasn't the rushes he heard before him but only their far-away whisper. It was the sea.

He ran again, not seeing but hearing. The wetness of the saltings grew louder beneath the soles of his trainers. A few hours ago this hadn't been land but water, and the dunes had been only islands. But now the sea had retreated and the land had followed, far out. And where it ended, he knew, he would find him.

He ran faster. The saltings slid away, back towards the dyke and the village, and the ground grew quiet where the tide hadn't reached it. Deeper now and tilting upward. He was on the dunes and his tread was like a deaf man's, moving but silent. The sand rose higher round his ankles. *Like clouds, only softer. Have you ever walked up clouds before?* Steeper here and too soft for walking. He dropped on all fours in the blackness and scrambled, clutching at the sand for support. But it trickled away like dry water, leaving his fingers empty. He lunged out again and his fist closed on grasses, cutting his palm like tin. He clung to them, pulling himself up against the slow sifting of the dune. Then the slope tipped him forward and had gone, plunging on ahead into space. From far out, the endless whisper rose to meet him and wind came with it, filling his tears with sand. He dragged himself to his feet and stood upright. Behind him and before him the dune slid again, then lay quiet. He was on the final ridge.

For a moment he paused, listening. The wind crept away and left him, and there was only emptiness. He was standing at the end of the world.

No, not yet. A bit farther yet. Out beyond the dunes, that's where it really ends.

The sea.

He flung himself blindly forward, stumbling down into deep dryness. His tears fell faster. Soon now. Out there, where the land ended.

The softness gave way and the dune was behind him. The beach grew solid, then sharp with the sound of breaking. He paused again, breathless, and the shells were silent. He knew where he was now. He'd been here before.

His cry rang out across the sightless darkness.

'Roly!'

His cry rang out across the gleaming darkness.

'Roly!'

No answer came. For a moment he remained where he was, blinking back tears. He turned his head. On either side the ribbon of shells narrowed away into night, waiting for the tide. He looked across the beach. The sand was wet with moonlight, shiny black. Beyond it, far out, another deeper blackness shone, rising and falling. Between the two, dividing black from black, a band of foam stretched endlessly away in both directions. He stared along it, knowing that it marked the ending of the land, the end of running. Roly could go no farther.

In the next instant, he saw him. He was there, far off to the left, where land and water met, the only point of shadow on the line of surf.

He cried out again and raced forward from the path of shells, diagonally across the beach. The sand grew damper as he ran, smooth at first then dipping into shallow pools of light, spraying up against his legs and hands. In quarter of a mile the land would be behind him.

'Roly!'

The distant figure hadn't moved. He could see him clearly now, dark against the shining of the water, turned away to seaward. The cries must have reached him, but he gave no sign of hearing.

The hollows of the beach grew deeper. Channels came, unexpected rifts and valleys slicing up the sand from sea to dunes, jolting at his body as they plunged him downward, ankle-high in water. Out there, where Roly stood, the sea seemed still withdrawn and sleeping. But here, beneath the land, its secret tide was waking and the channels were filling. Then they were behind him and the sand stretched out unbroken to the line of foam.

Step by step the beach fell back towards the dunes and vanished. The sea spread wider as he neared it, low against the land, with hidden waves far out that flexed beneath the surface, not breaking. Only its edge was loud and white with movement, dragging at the sand. He was close now. In another moment he would reach him.

The water slid towards him as he came, past Roly's feet and swiftly up the beach, then hissed away again in bubbles. He ran with it, half blind with salt and tears. Roly didn't turn to face him.

He tried to speak, but something choked his words and left him helpless. He reached out. The shoulder flinched beneath his hand, then stiffened. He clung to it, sobbing.

'Roly. . .'

Water slid again, sucking and retreating.

'Roly, it's me. . . I followed you. . . I had to.'

No answer came. Only the sea moved, cold across his feet and ankles. The ground shifted, sinking.

'Roly, please. Let's forget it. . . We can make it up, can't we? . . . Say something, Roly. . .'

Words thickened in his throat and stuck there. His hand spoke for him, tightening on the shoulder. He waited for the answer, the turning of the face towards his own. The answer came at last, but not the turning. The words hissed out to sea.

'Get away from me.'

'Roly, please.'

'Get away!'

'But why? What am I supposed to have done? Tell me.'

'Just get away from me, that's all!'

'I don't get it, Roly. What have I done?'

'Keep your filthy hands off me!'

'Roly, please.'

'Keep away from me, damn you!'

Roly swung, his face white with fury. He lashed out, thrusting him aside, and raced past him up the beach, leaving him to fall.

He fell, sprawling on the tide-line as Roly fled. The sand sagged open to receive him, then closed around his knees and fingers. The sea moved again, swift layers of water overlapping, sliding in to land and not retreating. The tide had turned. The sand dissolved beneath him. He scrambled to his feet and splashed ashore.

Roly was some way distant, heading for the dunes. He flung himself after, not knowing any longer if misery drove him forward or anger, only knowing he must catch him for the final time. The sand between them narrowed.

Halfway up the beach, he caught him. His hand closed on the jacket, wrenching it back towards him, swinging it round until both his fists took grip. For an instant Roly's nails clawed into his wrists and knuckles to break the hold he'd gained. He clung, unflinching. Then all resistance stopped. They stood there face to face in silence and fought for breath, not moving.

His own voice came at last, choking with tears and anguish.

'What's got into you, Roly, for God's sake?'

'Let go of me!'

'Come on, tell me!'

'Let go!'

'Pack it in, can't you, Roly! We're friends!'

The answer came in a single cry, ringing with mockery and laughter. 'Friends!'

'You know we are! You said so!'

'Look, how many more times do I have to tell you - it's finished!'

'No!' Anger sobbed from him now, sudden and uncontrolled. 'Who do you think you are anyway? Who the hell do you think you are? I suppose I'm not good enough for you any more! I suppose I've never been bloody good enough for you! Is that it? - Is it?'

'Yes!'

The word struck him like a blow. His hands lost their grip and fell away. He stood there in speechless horror, staring at the grinning face before him.

The grin widened. 'That's it! At last you've got it straight! Why the hell should I want you *as a friend?'*

'Roly, please. . .'

'Friends! You make me sick. You've always made me sick!'

'No! That's not true!'

'I hate the sight of you. If I had my way, you'd never see me again! So clear off! Just clear off back to the filthy scum where you belong! You're scum, d'you hear? Scum! Son of a bloody kitchen skivvy!'

With a final sneer of mockery Roly turned and left him, striding up towards the dunes. He saw him go, but didn't try to follow. The pain had gone now, and emptiness had come. It was over.

He stood there, unmoving. The figure grew darker as it went, merging with the darkness of the sand. Numbly, he watched. The shadow receded. He saw it stop. It hadn't reached the dunes. He heard the cry it gave. He didn't answer.

The distant figure faltered, then swung towards the right, chasing along the beach. It paused, retraced its steps, faster now, crossed towards the left. Again it stopped. Again the cry reached him.

The footsteps returned, grew louder, flew past him, seaward. He waited without turning, knowing that the cry would come once more. It came, from behind him, more desperate than before. The footsteps would come back now, towards him.

He heard the sound of their approach. And he heard the other sound that lay beyond them and around them, sweeping in from every side. From left and right it came, and downward from the darkness of the dunes. He knew what it was, but still he didn't move. It was the sound of the channels, the voice of the secret tide. Not secret any more, but open and triumphant, bursting from hiding to meet the oncoming sea.

The footsteps came nearer. Hushed now, drowned by the voice of water. But Roly's voice rose through it in a scream of terror, the lonely scream of terror of a boy who couldn't swim. The voice pierced his numbness, over and over. It was crying for protection. It was crying his name.

'TOM!'

His face streaming with tears, he turned and ran towards it.

Nineteen

Matthew was still standing on the line of shells. He hadn't moved. But he knew now. He'd remembered. He knew now what had happened on that final night, before he'd turned and run in answer to the cry. And after that. . . He shivered. That alone he didn't know, or want to.

He stirred uneasily, awaking broken echoes underfoot.

He'd been here before. He was standing where he'd stood once, long ago, before he'd crossed the beach to Roly. Beneath a hundred years of sand and tide the beach still held his footprints, racing out to sea and not returning. Soon now he would follow them once more.

He turned his head, unseeing, but knowing what he saw. Somewhere far out the same sea rose and fell, meeting the same land in endless foam. And where they met, the same small figure would be standing. But no longer as it was when last he'd looked from this same place and seen it, a distant point of shadow on the band of surf. This time, he knew, there'd be nothing there to show where Roly waited, for seeing eyes or blind ones. The ghost that he was now would cast no shadow.

Tears came again, hurting with the memory of what they'd spoken to each other in their final desperate meeting on the beach. Then another memory woke, a memory of the churchyard, and the words he'd cried at Roly by the grave. Yesterday. He listened, hearing them again.

Who the hell do you think you are anyway? I suppose our food's not good enough for you or something! I suppose we're not bloody good enough for you! Is that it?

And he understood at last the misery and terror that he'd heard in Roly's answer.

Don't say that! Don't ever say that again!

It had all happened before.

His tears had gone now, but not their hurting. He could hear it in the crying of his voice.

'Roly!'

His cry rang out to seaward and returned to him unanswered, then left him in the darkness on his own. For a moment more, he listened. A small wind crossed the sand and touched him, bringing word of weed and water. He must go now. It was time.

He moved. He left the place where he was standing, stumbling blindly forward, out across the beach. Faster now. He ran, knowing that his present footsteps followed older ones, long buried, though now he could see neither, old or new.

The sand grew damper as he ran, and smoother, then dipped and hollowed into stranded pools of spray. And deeper hollows came, and channels, ankle-high in water, slicing up the beach from sea to dunes. Then the splashing of his feet fell silent and the sand grew level, and he knew that he was close now to the end.

He tried to call but something choked the words inside him and his voice was only tears that wouldn't come. He listened as he ran, waiting for another voice to cry in answer. But no voice came. Nothing rose to meet him but the unseen water, loud with salt and foam. Louder now, and nearer. He stumbled on towards it.

It came at last. In a final rush of spray the ground dissolved beneath him and was gone. Breathless, he halted. Somewhere here, staring out to seaward, Roly would be standing. He'd reached the ending of the land now, the end of running. He could go no farther.

Again he tried to speak, fumbling forward into blackness,

hands outstretched. But no hands met his own and no voice answered. Only the sea moved, cold and empty, wanting nothing of him, giving nothing in return. Panic came, sudden and terrible. He'd come too late. The tide had turned, was sweeping in to land. Roly would have gone now, back beyond the saltings, would have left the beach behind him to the power of the sea. *You don't know it, Matt! You don't know it like I do! It scares me. I'm scared of its touch, scared of what it can do...*

He was here alone.

He stumbled backwards, floundering for balance. Water slid again, sucking and retreating, and the land slid with it, following out to sea. His heels were subsiding, dragging him downward into empty night. He toppled. His voice came at last, in a cry of terror. Then a second cry came. He heard it as he fell, ringing back towards him like a distant echo. But it wasn't an echo. He knew what he was hearing. It wasn't an echo but an answering call.

His head struck sand.

For a moment there was blackness, inside and out. Then his ears awoke. Footsteps were in them, louder and louder, racing towards him on the water's edge. He scrambled up and listened. Nearer now, and faster, and a voice was calling, shaken and bewildered as it cried his name. He turned and ran to meet it.

They met, as long ago. A hand reached out and held him though the voice had fallen silent, and he knew that the silence wasn't anger now, but tears.

'It's OK, Roly, it's OK now.'

The voice came at last, confused and broken.

'What's happening, Matt?... You can't be here... It's crazy.'

'I knew where you'd be – I had to come, I *had* to.'

'What's going on? You can't have known, you can't be here...'

'Roly, listen. *Please* listen. – It's OK now. It doesn't matter any more, about yesterday, about what happened. It's different now, it's all changed. We can start again now. . .'

'What're you on about, Matt? What're you *doing* here? You can't have got down here. . . I've gone crazy or something.'

He was trembling now, uncontrollably.

'Roly, you're not crazy. I'm trying to explain, you've got to let me try and explain. – I know now. I know everything.'

No sound came from Roly. His hand spoke for him, tightening in unbelieving horror on the arm it held.

'I know, Roly. I know everything that's happened. I've remembered about Tom.'

A spasm of agony contracted Roly's grip like a vice. Then the hand grew limp and fell away. They stood face to face, not breathing.

Roly's answer came through tears.

'It's not true. Tell me it's not true. You can't know. . .'

'Roly, you've got to believe me. I know what happened, all of it. I've remembered. I've been here before, haven't I? I know about us meeting, all that time ago. And I've come back now – I don't get how or why and I don't *care*, I just know I have, that's all. I understand now, about this week and us not having to be seen by anybody when we went out together in case they spoke to me and asked what I was doing on my own. I understand why you couldn't come to tea. I *know*, Roly. I know about you.'

He heard the stifled cry that Roly gave, heard him turn to run. He stumbled blindly after, clinging to him.

'Roly, *listen!* I know, and it's OK. I'm not scared of you. I wouldn't have come if I was scared.'

'Get away from me!'

Matthew heard the same words as long ago, and the same loathing. But this time, he knew, it wasn't him that Roly loathed. Roly only loathed himself.

'Can't you understand? I know, and I'm not scared.'

'Get away! Let go of me!'

'I know what you are, Roly, I *know*. You're a . . .'

The word stuck in his throat. With a cry, Roly swung back now, to face him.

'Go on then! If you're not scared, say it. Say what I am!'

'Roly. . .'

'Go on!'

'No!'

'Say it!'

'I can't!'

'Say it!'

'Roly, please. . . '

'*Say it, damn you!*'

'*All right! – You're a GHOST!*'

The word rang from him and echoed out into the night. Then silence came, and the slow movement of water. Roly made no sound now, but Matthew felt his sobbing.

'It's OK now, Roly. Nothing's changed. What difference is it supposed to make if people can't see you? Even if they could, it'd make no odds to me, I can't see *anybody*, can I? – We're still friends, aren't we, same as we always were.'

Roly's struggling had gone now. It was as if he'd collapsed.

'How can you say that after what happened? You can't know what happened and still say that.'

'I do know, I told you, and it makes no odds. I don't care, Roly. All that's finished now.'

Roly shivered suddenly, remembering.

'I didn't mean what I said, Matt. I was crazy that night. I don't know what made me say stuff like that to you. . .'

'Look, forget it, it's finished, like I said. I don't care about all that any more. We're going to start again, that's all. – You should've told me this week, Roly. You knew who I was, you should've told me. I'd have understood.'

'But I couldn't! Not after what happened! I hadn't got the right, not after that!'

'I don't get it, Roly. Why did you come to me at all then, if it wasn't so I'd know?'

'Don't you understand? I just wanted to show you things, that's all. I wanted to show you things like you showed them to me once. I thought it'd make up a bit for. . .' For an instant his voice broke, then rose again helpless with misery. 'I wanted to make it up to you, Matt!'

'Make what up for God's sake? It was a row, that's all. It wasn't your fault I followed you from the Hall that night, was it? It wasn't your fault what happened.'

'You can't say that – you can't say you know everything and still say that!'

'Look, it was just the tide. . .'

'You said you knew! You said you'd remembered!'

'I *have*. It was the tide. There wasn't anything we could do, it was too late. What difference does it make now? We couldn't swim, that's all.'

Roly seized him suddenly, gripping his shoulders.

'Can't you understand? It was me that couldn't swim. *Me!*'

A shudder crept up Matthew's spine, but he didn't know why.

'What're you on about?'

'You don't remember, do you! Not how it ended! You could've made it, Matt, you could've made it to the dunes.'

'It's not true!'

'You could swim! You tried to save me, you came back and tried to save me. I knew you could've got away but I wouldn't let you. . .'

'Please. . .'

'I was scared, Matt. I held on to you. It was my fault, all of it! I wouldn't let go!'

'*NO!*'

'Now do you see? Now do you see why I can't rest? – I've been here every day, Matt, every tide since then. I've watched it going out and leaving me behind, just wanting to go with it and be free. But I can't!'

Matthew stood, too cold for speaking now or moving, knowing at last. Somewhere deep inside him a memory of other words took shape. Mrs Weaver's words. *Ah yes, their bodies were found. Tom's had gone out with the tide, far out. But Rupert's was thrown back to shore, stranded when the tide turned and left it. They found it next day, lying among the shells. . .*

Then the crying of the other voice returned. And he knew it was the same voice that he'd heard as the gull had risen up from the water, the same cry.

'I told you, Matt, I hate the sea. I'm scared crazy of it, I know what it can do. But it's the only thing I've ever really wanted too. I want to be part of it. I want to go out with it. I want to rest!'

Still Matthew stood, and gave no answer. He'd remembered now, the final horror. But dimly, for the first time, he knew that even now he hadn't reached the ending. Something more horrible was yet to come. Not something from the past but something now, in the present. Something he'd been brought here to do.

He heard his own voice speaking and knew that it was lying, to keep away a truth he couldn't face.

'It's OK, Roly, it's all finished now. We can't change all that. But we can forget it, can't we? We can start again.'

Roly's hands tightened on his shoulders, though his voice was quiet.

'Matt, listen to me. It's not finished, you know it's not, not for me. I couldn't have told you all this before, you'd have been as scared as hell. I didn't come to you this week to tell you, I swear I didn't. I hadn't got the right. I just wanted to make it up to you a bit, that's all. I even tried to keep it from you when I saw you'd guessed whose room it was, up at the top of the Hall. But you've found out now, you've been brought back here to find out, on your own. You've been brought back here to help me. And you've got to help me,

Matt, you've *got* to.'

'It'll be OK, Roly, you'll see. I don't care what happened. I'll come back here again, I promise, every holiday. We can be together now. . .'

'Matt, please. . .'

'We've got to go now. Take me back. I'm scared, Roly. I can't see.'

'Listen to me. . .'

'Come on, Roly, I can't stay here. You know I can't.'

'Can't you understand? You've got to help me!'

'I can't!'

'It's my last chance!'

'Take me home, Roly. *Please*. I don't like it here, it's like last time. The tide's coming in!'

'It's not, Matt, not this time! You can feel it's not! It's going out!'

'No!'

But his feet told him that Roly's words were true. The water had gone from them, and the land had come. Roly's face was near his own now, his quiet voice urgent with tears.

'It's going out. You know it is. Let me go with it. Let me be free.'

'I can't help you. There's nothing I can do!'

'You know that's not true, you know you can free me.'

'I don't know what you're on about, Roly. I'm scared.'

'Say it, Matt – say what you've been brought here to say.'

'Pack it in, can't you? Let's go now. . .'

'Say it!'

'I don't get it, Roly. I don't know what you want with me. . .'

'You do know! You don't want to say it! But you've got to! You can't keep me here like this, you can't!'

'You've *got* to stay. I *want* you to stay. We're friends!'

Roly held to him, sobbing.

'Matt, listen. You go home today. The tide's on the turn. It's the only chance I've got. I can't tell you what words to speak, I can't make you say them. They've got to come from *you.* But you know why I'm still here, you know what I did to you. You know the words that'll free me. – Say them, Matt, before it's too late!'

'No! I don't want you to leave me!'

Roly tensed suddenly, and Matthew knew that the face had turned from him. He followed it seaward, listening with it. The sound of the waves had changed. Their retreating whisper had ceased now. The sea was suspended, poised on the silence between ebb-tide and flood-tide. The water was holding its breath.

Soon now, it would be over.

He clung to the helpless figure before him as he had once clung to another, as if to stop it moving away. And the words Mrs Weaver had spoken then returned like a far-away echo. *Times change, and we must just accept them. We can't hold on to things for ever, can we? Let them go, Matthew, when you have to...*

Roly wrenched himself away. His footsteps were running to the sea. Then they stopped. In the silence, his voice sobbed back.

'Please – the tide's going to turn! It's my only chance! I'm sorry what I did, Matt, I'm sorry what happened. I've tried to make it up, I really have. Say you understand.'

'I can't!'

'I've got to go now, I've got to leave you. Say the words, Matt. Let me go!'

'I can't!'

'Say them!'

'No!'

'The tide, Matt, listen! Say the words! Please!'

'Roly...'

'*Please!*'

'Roly... *I FORGIVE YOU!*'

A cry came ringing from before him, in answer to his own.

He heard it piercing the darkness, and knew at last what it told him. It was a cry of joy. And he thought he saw. The gull rose up from the water. And it was as if Roly's hand was once more on his shoulder, guiding his eyes to the wind. *Do you know what people say about the gulls, do you know what they say they are? They say they're souls, Matt. Risen souls.* But this time he knew that Roly was no longer with him.

For an instant the cry seemed to linger, as if the bird was wheeling before him in a flurry of brightness. Then it faded away and was gone.

When Matthew reached the top of the dune he paused and wiped his sleeve across his face. He looked back. The shadows on his eyes remained unbroken, shadows of sand and sea. But lighter than they'd been beside the water. The dark had gone now. Day was almost here.

A wind came creeping in to land and touched him. He closed his eyes against it. And though his eyes were closed he knew what he was seeing, the marks he'd left behind him on the sand. His own footprints, racing out towards the water and coming back to land.

He turned his head. With eyes still closed, he scanned the beach to westward. He knew what he would find there. Another set of footprints leading outward, ending at the tide-line, not returning. He smiled. They looked so strange. People would wonder, if they saw them. They looked as if they'd left the land behind them and just gone on and on across the sea, not stopping, ever.

INTO THE DARK

Book covers from earlier editions

First English Edition
Cover artwork by Alun Hood

ISBN 0-00-184426-1
9 780001 844261

First English Paperback
Cover artwork by David Kearney

Second English Paperback

First American Edition
Cover artwork by E. T. Steadman

51295
9 780590 434249
ISBN 0-590-43424-1

First Danish Edition

First Spanish Edition

First Italian Edition

SUPERJUNIOR

HORROR

Brivido, tenebre e mistero, fantasmi e creature della notte per chi ama la "paura da leggere" e ha superato la soglia dei 12 anni.

Ombre
Chi vive nel buio, come Matthew, deve affidarsi al tatto, all'udito, all'odorato, e, naturalmente, all'aiuto degli altri. Matthew, però, ha anche un'altra risorsa: pur essendo cieco riesce a vedere ciò che altri non vedono e ad entrare in contatto con immagini del passato. Ma tutto questo lo scoprirà soltanto attraverso il rapporto con uno strano ragazzo, Roly, che in un certo senso è anche lui una creatura del buio, e che ha un disperato bisogno di aiuto. E solo Matthew, tra tutti, può davvero aiutarlo, in nome di una amicizia che sembra aver sfidato il tempo e lo spazio. Una storia sommessa e piena di atmosfera, scritta da un maestro della *ghost story* inglese.

Nicholas Wilde è uno scrittore inglese che insegna a Cambridge. Scrive e illustra i suoi libri e molto del suo tempo libero lo occupa dedicandosi a collezionare libri per bambini.

Illustrazione di copertina di Angelo Stano

Lire 12.000

In Italy, *Into the Dark* was called *Shadows*. The synopsis on the back cover reads: "Anyone who lives in the dark, as Matthew does, must trust to touch, hearing and smell, and of course to the help of others. Matthew, however, has another resource: because of his blindness he can also see what other people are unable to, and make contact with images of the past. But all this will be revealed to him only through his relationship with a strange boy, Roly, who in a certain sense is also a creature of the dark who has a separate need of help. And in all the world it is only Matthew who can really help him, in the name of a friendship which seems to have defied both time and space. A subtle and atmospheric novel by a master of the English 'ghost story'. "

Reviews

"The story of a boy's emergence from dependency... the discovery of the necessity of forgiveness; the acceptance of pain and the release of a chained spirit. It operates on many different levels but its greatest strength lies in the vivid descriptions of a boy's experience. The final chapters reach a poetic level. Its nearest equivalent is *Red Shift* by Alan Garner in its sensitive understanding of the feelings of young people." *The Essex Review*

"An unusually tense story. . . The haunted style and effect are well suited to the plot." Jacqueline Simms, *Times Literary Supplement*

"Rich in suspense and atmosphere." Douglas Hill, *The Guardian*

"*Into the Dark* is about ways of seeing ... an environment of sea and saltmarsh, a suitably bare and timeless landscape for this story of youthful loneliness and longing. The author's finest achievement is in creating a realistic contemporary atmosphere and weaving this convincingly into his plot."
Robert Dunbar, *Times Educational Supplement*

"... deftly combines a supernatural theme with sympathetic insights into the life of a twelve-year-old boy. The power and immediacy of the writing, the skilfully drawn characters and the subtle supernatural elements make this a moving and absorbing read." L. N. *Books for Keeps*

"*Into the Dark* is a British ghost story in the tradition of Lucy Boston's *Green Knowe* books. It has evocative writing, well-developed characters, a distinctive setting, and the skilful mingling of the past and present." Julie Corsaro, *Booklist USA*

"A haunting story which is unfolded so beautifully. This book is a treasure." *Books for Children*, Reviewer's top choice

"A first-rate mystery writer with an extraordinary ability to create a feeling of tension within a good, strong storyline. It is unusual to find an author whose next book is awaited with such anticipation... *Into the Dark* is a superb story which the reader is sorry to finish." Margaret Hobson and Jennifer Madden, *The Children's Fiction Sourcebook*

"The clues come to us early ... and the climax is memorable." Naomi Lewis, *The Observer*

Lightning Source UK Ltd.
Milton Keynes UK
UKHW010728301121
394820UK00010B/639/J